Sound of an Iceberg

NEW WRITING SCOTLAND 37

Edited by
Susie Maguire
and
Samuel Tongue

Gaelic adviser:
Rody Gorman

Association for Scottish Literary Studies

Association for Scottish Literary Studies
Scottish Literature, 7 University Gardens
University of Glasgow, Glasgow G12 8QH
www.asls.org.uk

ASLS is a registered charity no. SC006535

First published 2019

British Library Cataloguing in Publication Data

A CIP record for this book is available
from the British Library

ISBN 978-1-906841-39-3

The Association for Scottish Literary Studies
acknowledges the support of Creative Scotland
towards the publication of this book

Printed by Bell & Bain Ltd, Glasgow

CONTENTS

INTRODUCTION

As I write this introduction to issue 37 of *New Writing Scotland* a 'No-Deal Brexit' is the iceberg floating ever closer to the puttering ship of state and the displacement caused by its weight dominates the political horizon. Although it's questionable that this particular ship is as graceful or seaworthy as the *Titanic* of Thomas Hardy's haunting poem 'The Convergence of the Twain', we are certainly 'bent / By paths coincident' to meet this sinister 'Shape of Ice'.

Given the political tumult through which we are living and the social media sprint of news and outrage, by the time you read this, it will almost certainly sound belated. And of course, all of the writing collected here was produced before No. 10's current incumbent took to the despatch box. Print media is slow media. But within the word *read,* the connotations of past, present, and future jostle for priority. To read is to have read. The best writing manages to remain within these tensions, framing a moment in time, even creating time in writing itself, but also speaking to readers still distant. This is part of literature's magic. Reading slowly, carefully, can be an antidote to the harassment and tyranny of the 24/7 political news cycle. Stay informed, yes; all the writing here is informed and, in every case, informative. But what in-*forms* us? Alycia Pirmohamed's poem 'Ebb and Flow' plays on the fact that, if our bodies are watery forms we must also 'be / almost a river'. The stories and poems collected here are tributaries, streams, burns, and rivers flowing into the oceanic depths of our consciousness, where the wreck of the *Titanic* still sits, heavy in the dark.

Karen Ashe's poem 'The Sound of an Iceberg, Calving' inspired the title of this issue and it conjures with some of Hardy's dread, updating it for an age of 'super-fast fibre-optic wifi'.

> It's more a soft whump,
> then an elegant leaving, like

a grand piano dropped
from a silent-movie window,
a slow-motion school bus
over a soap-opera cliff

The poem skilfully blends hints of environmental collapse with hyper-consumerism, shadowed by a generalised anxiety that permeates much of the writing here (that 'soap-opera cliff' edge is certainly an image to conjure with). Indeed, last year's issue of *NWS* was castigated in the *Scottish Review of Books* for displaying 'little *joie de vivre*'. Perhaps it is a sign of the times, but Susie and I cannot claim that this issue will be a barrel of laughs either. Yet there is always hope in the dark times – in Henry Bell's poem 'Dear Scottish Poets from England', Scotland is a country where poets and writers can find a place to work and to build. Without dismissing the fraught and necessary debates on the power of institutional gatekeepers, is there a possibility for other kinds of imagined communities, 'unions' made across the nations of the UK *and* internationally through the arts, that are able to swerve from the chaos that Westminster politics will continue to mete out? Perhaps this is redolent with magical thinking – you can read Dan Spencer's story 'Our Common Areas' for an antidote to ideas of community-as-utopia.

The tagline for this year's *La Biennale di Venezia* is 'May you live in interesting times'. Is this proverb a curse or a blessing? Reading through the 500-plus submissions for this issue, many writers shuttle between the two; when the selected pieces come together in the volume you now hold, our 'interesting' times are refracted through many different perspectives, and as a collective, they refuse to decide the question. The immediate future certainly looks 'interesting' as we examine the glittering malevolence or sunlit optimism reflected in the multifaceted Brexit iceberg. But the writers collected here are doing more than rearranging the deckchairs as the iceberg floats closer – they are informing our thoughts and actions, and providing possibilities for thinking things differently. I am already looking forward to the next tranche of submissions, papery lifeboats on which to cast ourselves, not to escape, but to take another view.

This issue marks the last for my co-selector Susie Maguire. I cannot thank her enough for her wit, comradeship, and editorial eagle-eye through our two issues together. I have enjoyed our commentaries, conversations and compromises very much. Duncan Jones and Margaret Renton were, as ever, unstinting in their work for *NWS* and ASLS, coming through in some financially trying times. It takes many hands to keep this particular boat afloat and our thanks go to all.

Samuel Tongue

NEW WRITING SCOTLAND 38: SUBMISSION INSTRUCTIONS

The thirty-eighth volume of *New Writing Scotland* will be published in summer 2020. Submissions are invited from writers resident in Scotland or Scots by birth, upbringing or inclination. All forms of writing are welcome: autobiography and memoirs; creative responses to events and experiences; drama; graphic artwork (monochrome only); poetry; political and cultural commentary and satire; short fiction; travel writing or any other creative prose may be submitted, but not full-length plays or novels, though self-contained extracts are acceptable. The work must not be previously published, submitted, or accepted for publication elsewhere, and may be in any of the languages of Scotland.

Submissions should be typed on one side of the paper only and the sheets secured at the top left corner. Prose pieces should be double-spaced and carry an approximate word-count. **You should provide a covering letter, clearly marked with your name and address. *Please also put your name on the individual works*.** If you would like to receive an acknowledgement of receipt of your manuscript, please enclose a stamped addressed postcard. If you would like to be informed if your submission is unsuccessful, or would like your submissions returned, you should enclose a stamped addressed envelope with sufficient postage. Submissions should be sent by **31 October 2019**, in an A4 envelope, to the address below, or online via **Submittable** at **nws.submittable.com/submit**. We are sorry but we cannot accept submissions by email.

Please be aware that we have limited space in each edition, and therefore shorter pieces are more suitable – although longer items of exceptional quality may still be included. **Please send no more than four poems, or one prose work**. Successful contributors will be paid at the rate of £20 per published page. Authors retain all rights to their work(s), and are free to submit and/or publish the same work(s) elsewhere after they appear in *New Writing Scotland*.

ASLS
Scottish Literature
7 University Gardens
University of Glasgow
Glasgow G12 8QH, Scotland
www.asls.org.uk

James Aitchison

IN AITKEN'S STABLES

On my way to the children's library
in Hope Street almost seventy years ago
I'd stop by a window – at pavement level, barred –
of Aitken's Falkirk Brewery and look down
at the Clydesdales stabled underground.

They stood upright but with lowered heads;
Aitken's horses were sleeping on their feet.

From November to March in the early-evening dark
the dim-lit underworld outshone the street.
The sleeping horses were far away and yet –
a glint of metal from a tilted hoof –
they were closer, bigger than they were by day.

There were evenings when I didn't know
I'd been kneeling until I stood up again.

Karen Ashe

THE SOUND OF AN ICEBERG   CALVING

It's not the crack you expect.
It's more a soft whump,
then an elegant leaving, like
a grand piano dropped
from a silent-movie window,
a slow-motion school bus
over a soap-opera cliff,
Falling Man falling
forever on prime-time news
then the kettle clicks to a rapid boil
as a small finger presses a button,
the screen flickers and blurs,
and the iceberg is replaced
by slimming ads and payday loans,
super-fast fibre-optic wifi,
high-speed trains, and the tea
bleeds into the water and milk
delivered unseen in early hours
from cows in distant misty pastures
stays fresh for nine days
in fat plastic bottles
that go in the recycling
and the baby shudders inside
half a month from completion
and the buy-now-pay-later sofa
is wobbly in the leg already
and the interest-free 42-inch telly is frozen
on an ad for wonga.com
and the dunked biscuit dissolves
in the tea in the time it takes

to change channels
and in some faraway dark cold country
of slavering bears and wandering herdsmen
the iceberg
is still
calving.

Pamela Beasant

LEAVING

As the coast of Australia slips away,
picked out in sharp relief
past the wing tip,
we head over a perfect
tile of ocean, back in time,
and I will take
a little piece of strange
beauty, and the faces,
especially yours,
looking at me intently
through the camera lens,
and when I watch seagulls
quarrelling in Stromness
I'll imagine flocks of
cockatoos, and cows will become,
for an instant, kangaroos,
and the moon that waxed
in Wollongong and Canberra
revealing a strange geography
will reflect light
on both our upturned faces.

Henry Bell

DEAR SCOTTISH POETS FROM ENGLAND

Dear Scottish poets from England,
I see you
hiding your Essex under a bushel.
Sharpening your consonants,
flattening your vowels,
trying to brush off
those first ten years in London
like so much ash on your sleeve.

Dear Scottish poets from England
I see you
discussing weekends in Devon
in hushed tones, denying
all knowledge of cricket,
carrying a chip on your shoulder
just that little bit larger
than the Scottish Scottish poets'.

O Scottish poets from England
let me join your:
glaikit eyes torn between Williams
Wallace and Morris; dancing at ceilidhs
in an invisible bowler hat; devouring
Mitchell and Morgan. Across the multiverse
the poets have no country,
and Scotland is a good place to start.

Eloise Birtwhistle

WHOLEHEARTED

In the right atrium my mother is on a boat
At the stern, vowels elongate
from South Africa to Southampton
where their wake dissolves
into an accent that fits in at school
Gogo has Nelson Mandela on her fridge
we tease her when she says fuk awf

My father in the right ventricle
misses London and the British Library
says white so you hear the h
His language speaks from the page
in the voice of your inner ear
When I was fourteen he gave me Yeats
and marked the poems he knew I'd hear

With the squeeze also comes the push
Blood pump from heart to lung
blood breathe external airs
oxidise with new sounds
that give delight and hurt not
Re-entering the left atrium it brings
the vowels, the syllables, the slang of Sheffield

In the pitch and pace of staccato Glasgow
flow calms, sound neutralises
Crossing the border into the left ventricle
those Yorkshire vowels shallow from gullet to mouth
speech becomes something unplaceable
chambers resonate with nowhere
manywhere

Blood rushes onward through body
beat to stomach, brain, fingertip
slip in and out with geography
audience, emotion, sobriety
Each chamber keeping time
Lips filled many red when you ask me
about the language of my heart

Chris Boyland

ANDERSTON

Young men climb wearily to the
    tops of once-existent towers,
stairs lapping around their feet, waves
    coming in, waves going out

Telephones ring out of an empty sky,
    birds with voices of long-dead
callers, sing querulous songs about the
    state of the world today

Streetlights muzzled by shadows cast
    by nothing, no shapes loom
behind the angled dark, nothing comes
    of nothing, nothing grows

Pavements turn upon themselves,
    catch pedestrians unawares,
suddenly indoors, suddenly behind
    since-demolished walls

The sky is a ceiling, abruptly and
    emphatically lowered, bearing
down with all the weight of an architect's
    brutalist righteousness

New towns in the distance, circle
    the wounded city like wolves
around a dying ox, waiting to feast on
    its rich and tender throat

Seems the moon is concrete, seems the
    stars are born aloft on monstrous
pillars, leaving footprints in the red earth,
    in the dear green earth

Carcasses of bus stations, dream
    of suffrage of old ideas and days
when they will wake and dance fandangos
    on insectile feet

Seems the death of buildings
    is not an end.

Sam Burns

THIS IS THE REFRAIN

for Patrick and Jacqueline Morreau

This is the refrain: 'Are you my husband?
I don't know anything these days. I love you.'
'Quite right,' he says, not one for wasting words.

Without a sigh he packs away the sunlit
summer days he saved for twilit winter evenings.
'I don't know anything these days. I love you.'

He lifts her from the chaise, a stringless puppet;
a swaddled Venus. He bathes her in those
summer days he saved for twilit winter evenings.

'Who's that?' she asks her portrait of their daughter,
reclining, bundled, coddled, loved, adoring;
a swaddled Venus. He bathes her in those

forgotten worlds the years have stripped away.
'I'm here, aren't I?' He strokes her hand. She stills,
reclining, bundled, coddled, loved, adoring.

Her love spills from her twenty times a day;
this is the refrain. 'Are you my husband?'
'I'm here, aren't I?' He strokes her hand. She stills.
'I don't know anything these days.' I love you.

Norman Coburn

SLICK O WID

It begins on a miserable Friday night. Wind howling from the east, aiming bullets of snow into our faces. Taking the dog out is our only concession to a late winter's day spent indoors. We walk to where the coastal streetlights hold the border against a hostile blackness beyond. Before we can stop him, the dog is down in the surf wrestling a plank. Along the shoreline, I can see two more pieces of wood.

'That's your best jacket,' she calls after me, more in hope than expectation I'll leave three good timbers until the morning. I offer her one to carry back, but she says, 'No thank you.'

Suit yourself. But the fire doesn't just burn fresh air.

Saturday morning brings another half dozen sizeable panels up onto the beach. I add them to my stash. And it not as if I'm the first one down. These ones are too good for burning. My mind turns to jobs I'll get done with a decent piece of wood. A man I don't know well greets me with a knowing smile.

By evening there's a buzz about the town.

Hushed conversations in pubs. Facebook messages exchanged between acquaintances. Rumours about a ship shedding its load in the Humber. Three days of strong easterly winds pushing this bounty towards our shore. Vans are made ready. Friends, and friends of friends. Even sons are primed.

We'll be down again at first light to see what the overnight tide brings us.

My boy grumbles as I rouse him for the third time. Cresting the raised beach we can see vehicles and groups of men at work. I'm thinking we've missed out. Then I look at the sea. The summit of every wave carries boards up to five metres long. Wind overpowers the retreating tide to push them toward us. An old friend strides past us and winks at me. He's been hard at work among a group of people who seem to be experts at this kind of thing. Guys in joiners' vans, selecting the best pieces; ignoring the trash. A bear of a man, thickly bearded, thigh-deep in the water, hoists boards through the air like missiles. We dive in among them. In moments we have as much as we can carry and make off with our share.

The afternoon brings a rising tide and at last, all the pieces, the whole pattern of planks and splinters, are thrust upon the shore. The heaviest pieces, laggards in the race to the beach, now push in behind the flotsam. Scaffolding panels crash, like aircraft carriers, through flotillas of smaller craft. And now we're ready for them. The East Fife villages are ready to fill their boots.

And everyone comes.

Someone shows me a photo taken earlier at Fife Ness. 'It's lyin' waist deep out there.' The pile in the image is impressive, but too neatly stacked to be beach wrack. Another old man with a fag tacked to his lips announces he's done for the day. He's had eighty pieces already, he tells me. Looking at his stringy body, I'm not sure I believe him. However, the beach is his advocate. Boards land upon boards as the last force of the storm pushes the wreck into our hands. More dance in the surf, hanging out of reach until the sea decides to ground them.

By dinnertime, it's going like a fair.

Vans, barrows, bicycles. I see someone using the frame of an old Silver Cross, dragged down from its attic and burdened with timbers where babies once lay. Together we go at it with a gusto that would make us world famous, if only we were rescuing refugees. Working in families, in groups of friends. Forming chains between surf and dry land, each crew with its own stack.

My son and I throw our lot in with a group of neighbours. Having agreed terms we re-join the fray.

A flatbed truck pulls up with a gang of lads. Its Kirkcaldy livery raises howls of derision from the beach and the interlopers find themselves faced off by Dyker men ten times their number.

The foxes put their tails between their legs and retreat to find easier pickings.

The harbour master flits among the groups, soliciting anxious nods. 'Stay off the sea, lads. There's not a boat in Anster could make it through that slick o wid.'

Another man, connected to the lifeboat I think, holds hushed, urgent conversations. The groups redirect their efforts to fetching the piles into waiting vehicles. 'The Receiver of Wrecks has been called. This whole lot might yet be impounded.'

Not a soul can bear to miss their share in the spoil. Is it greed, or can I no longer see past the splint in my own eye? I see a young couple with three long planks between them. And I wonder what they'll do with their prize, living as they do on the fourth floor of the tenement.

And them with no garden!

I know an old lady who'd lived on Skye. Growing up during the war, she and some friends once came upon a beach scattered with tennis balls. She remembers how the children laughed and played, bravely hiding their disappointment as these new toys quickly disintegrated into sticky piles. A mother came down to the beach to chase a tardy child. Realising the spoils were in fact oranges, she called for her kin to gather this long-forgotten delicacy. And while much of it was shared, too much rotted in the larders of the greedy.

Back in the now, children gasp and point.

Two hundred feet above this shore of human effort, a coastguard helicopter roars overhead and out to sea. The slick is several miles long and fragmenting. As deadly to small craft as oil can be to birds.

As the evening tide recedes, so does the remaining driftwood. Back out to sea, ready to bless another beach on another day. I stand talking with a friend and we imagine this is how it feels to survive a battle. To be among the last men standing. Exulted, exhausted, hands bleeding. Beside me, this old warrior, well familiar with hard work, is so tired he cannot lift his arms higher than his chest. And yet, tomorrow, if the same opportunity presents, he'd do it all over again.

Word gets around the wreck's been declared a total loss. An insurance company will pick up the tab. This means the Exciseman will have no cause to walk our streets and vennels in the days to come. The mood eases and the banter turns sharper. Talk of extensions, of sheds and summer houses. Of one godly family with enough wood to build an ark.

I watch the last of them trudge away from the beach, to bars and kitchens. In this moment I have the sense of having slipped back through time. To a community once again united in a common effort, taking its great harvest, from the wealth of the sea.

Krishan Coupland

MORE A HEADBUTT THAN A KISS

You're my favourite pupil, I tell her. In the car park above the beach she fiddles with her bra, hands doglegged behind her back, tongue between teeth in concentration. Her body's still young for her, not yet rid of that skinny teenage awkwardness. She moves like a foal walks. In her earlobe there's this little plastic spacer. I touch it and ask where she got it from.

This shop in town, she says. *Snap*. Her bra comes off. She looks nervously around, but the beach is always empty this time of day. Am I really your favourite?

Yes, I say. But you can't drive for shit. After that we don't talk for a while. Rustling. And breaths. She only ever had one boyfriend before, she says, but I don't believe a word. She can lie when she wants to. She's good at it, even.

On the way back to her house I let her drive. Three or four times I have to use the brake, and once I lean over and grab the wheel so that she doesn't steer us into a bollard. She goes bright red and under her breath says sorry, sorry, sorry. And I say, don't be. I sign her little card and take her money, which is really her parents' money.

She doesn't look back as she disappears into the house. I get out, walk around the front of the car and get in the driver's side. It feels quieter here now, without her. Still smells of condoms, slick and greasy. The seat still warm. I adjust it back, and drive home slowly with the radio on.

I wash the car. Clean inside with the little vacuum. I put dinner in the oven and sit down to wait.

*

She is seventeen. Samantha. Seventeen and three months, and she wants to be a pharmacist. Small tits. Skinny arms. Bites her lip when she's trying to concentrate. Bites her lip so much that there's forever a small red puncture at the corner of her mouth. She's growing her hair and it's too long, at the moment, to look intentional. Sometimes she wears intricate little braids in a crown around the top of her head.

She dresses up for me. I can tell. The smell of girl deodorant accompanies her into the car, powdery and clean. There're always lines around her eyes, dark flicked tails at each corner. I said I liked her bra once (a white one, patterned with ropes and anchors), and now she wears it every time. Her cunt is small, and she keeps the hair there trimmed to a short fuzz. Her legs are strong, her hips flat. My favourite part of her is the place, smooth and muscular, between her breasts and her belly. When I touch her there she shivers, the whole of her, and her voice goes high and quiet.

*

Next week she gets in and says, can we go somewhere fun today? I make her drive all the way to the car park. She's still half-shocked and half-excited by the word fuck. It's over quickly. Seriously, she says, I want to go somewhere nice. Can we go to the arcade again, like before?

The arcade is empty too. Everyone has jobs or school. I change a twenty and we waste it all. It's so noisy I can barely hear her when she speaks. With the last pound on the claw machine she wins an Angry Bird.

Oh my god, I love these. She snatches it and hugs it. Its squashed face peers from between her arms, frowning and confused. Will you keep it? she says. I can't take it back. Will you keep it safe?

I let it sit on the dashboard, stuffed down in the corner so it won't roll around. It glares at me steadily with wide white cartoon eyes, poky wings just stubs sticking out of an obese body.

I can't believe it, she says. I've never won anything before. I *never* win anything. There's just time, in the little underground car park behind the solicitor's office. The Angry Bird watches me, frowning, disapproving. I want to reach out and turn it around so that it frowns out of the window instead, but I can't reach it from where I am, and so I shut my eyes instead.

After I finish she says, I don't want today to end. It's been so good. I wonder about the boys at her school. If she fucks them. If she wants to. Perhaps she has a bright young boyfriend somewhere who can't wait to touch her, who's never seen her naked but longs for it daily, who'd give everything to do one tiny portion of what I do to her.

Because we've overrun the lesson, I drive back and drop her off. She waves to me just before she disappears inside the house, and I put the car in gear again.

The next weekend is my turn to have Ben. Last time I promised I'd take him to the cinema, but I'm hoping by now he'll have forgotten. He climbs in and does up his seatbelt. I pat his head. How's Mum? I say, and he says, good. Are we going to watch a film today, Dad? You said we could go watch a film.

Sure, I say. Why not? Halfway to the cinema he sees the Angry Bird and he grabs it and starts flying it around the car.

Is it for me? he says. He's only young still and wants everything to be for him.

Of course it's for you, I say, but it has to live in the car, okay? You can't take it out with you. This is its home.

He nods seriously. He hugs it all the way to the cinema, but when it's time to come out he tucks it back in the corner. I fall asleep during the film and wake up to Ben pulling on my sleeve. I can't make sense of what he's saying at first. It smells of spilled slushy in the auditorium, and the lights are up. Around us everyone is murmuring and rustling. A baby crying somewhere at the back. He looks worried, Ben does. My son does. His small face screwed up with puzzlement, trying to understand. He's very beautiful.

Sorry, I say. I fell asleep.

When Ben is around I set up the sofa bed and leave the hallway light on. He's too old for it really, but his mother won't let him have a light on and I will, and that's important. I make him hot milk and put animal crackers on a plate.

When she comes to collect him she waits at the bottom of the drive. That's what she always does. Waits with the engine running and calls the house phone so that it rings once to let me know she's there. I pack up all his stuff in the little backpack and send him out, watch him walk down the drive, through no-man's land, away to that big car. I can't see beyond the tinted windows. The most I catch is a glimpse of pale-white skin as she reaches across him to pull shut the door.

I start drinking as soon as he's gone. That's what the weekends are for: Ben and vodka. Otherwise the evening starts to seem really long and the day ends up unbalanced, with everything crowded together in the morning and nothing at all between then and night. There's something on television, but it doesn't really matter what. A show about a wedding where they're having trouble with the cake. That, I think, is just the start of their problems.

Half-eight the phone rings. I backtrack (standing, feeling my head almost tip off my shoulders, scrabbling for the light switch or my phone or my keys) and it's only been a handful of hours since Ben climbed into the car and disappeared.

Hello? It's Samantha, and she wants to know where I am. It's all confused. I flip through my leather bound appointment book, trying to make my eyes make sense, and there she is. *8PM, S, 1H*. It must be a mistake though; I never do lessons on weekends. That's my time. Mine and Ben's.

Of course, I say, I'll be right over. I hang up and look around for my keys. It's so dark; it takes me ages to figure out I need to turn on the light. I dig in the crevices of the sofa, then up to the bathroom to splash water on my face. It feels like oil, clinging to my skin and refusing to drip away. I shake myself. There's a missed call on my phone.

Sorry about that, I say when she climbs in beside me. Things got away from me a bit.

It's okay, she says. It's good to see you.

I sit back and let her drive. It's quiet enough. We sit at junctions for almost a minute each time, and my head throbs whenever we go too fast over a speed bump. But then we stop and I look up and she's taken us to the car park above the beach. I feel my guts fighting each other but I manage to get out in time. Sick splashes my shoes.

You're ill, she says. I must stink. She's standing back with one arm crossed over her chest. She never knows what to do with her arms and I love that about her. Like watching a baby deer walking for the first time. She pats me on the back. Come on, she says, get back in the car.

I'm worse than I thought I was. We sit with the doors open for a little while and I wonder if she's disappointed. Have I disappointed her? Would it be worse if I hadn't? I try to explain by telling her about Ben and about how I don't usually do lessons at the weekend and she just nods, gripping the wheel.

I . . . I can take you home? she says. And she does. I keep the window halfway open so that cold air moves over my face and I can breathe and I can see. Samantha's driving even more careful now, as if scared she's going to make me sick again. Every time she misses a turning in the dark she says sorry. Sorry, sorry, sorry.

You're not the one who should be apologising, I say. Or I try to say, but the words come out wrong, just a mumble.

I have to give her my keys because I can't do it myself. She goes in first and pads around kicking over shoes and feeling the wall for a switch. Come on now, she says. On our way down the hall she looks at everything. The pictures and the coats. Even peers into the overflowing bin underneath the telephone table.

The door holds me up while she sweeps everything off the couch. Some of it – the takeaway boxes and old receipts – goes in the bin, and the rest she piles up at the foot of the sofa. It feels good to lie down. It feels right. Little hands unlace my shoes and pull them away. I wonder if my feet smell of sweat.

Where's the kitchen? she says, I'll get you some water.

When she comes back it's with a big pitcher full of tap water, and some toast. I didn't even know that I had bread. She sits down on the sofa just level with my stomach, as though she intends to feed me, but then gives me the plate and watches as I eat. It's good. It settles the churning in my stomach and makes me thirsty enough to drink half the water.

Better? she says. It must be past her lesson time now, but she's just sitting there calmly.

You should call your parents, I say.

They're out.

She strokes my hair. I wouldn't normally let her, but it feels good. Feels as though she actually does care a little. Sleepy now, and she lies down alongside me on the sofa, and we arrange ourselves. I end up hugging her against my chest because it's the only way we can both fit. Samantha's hair smells of mint. I'm so big compared to her: tiny hands and tiny head and tiny little body. I'm like a giant. That's how I must seem.

In the morning she's still there, unshakeably asleep. I wake first and lie there watching her breathe, feeling dry and washed out, like a towel where the ticking's wearing thin. A little string of drool hangs from her mouth to the sofa cushion. I was so sure that she would leave. My head's not as bad as I thought it would be; the water did some good after all.

The house is a mess. Bottles crowded on the windowsill like translucent soldiers. Cabinets streaked with the drool of over-heated ready meals. It stinks of body, like a changing room, but it's too late to change any of it. She's seen it now. I draw a glass of water from the tap and take it back into the lounge and watch her sleeping. I was *certain* that she would leave. So far, she's the only one who hasn't.

Samantha, I say. I have to touch her shoulder to make her come awake. She rubs her eyes and smudges the black around them so it looks like bruise.

Are you okay? she says. I feel like crying.

You need to get home, I say. Come on. I help her up. Her body is soft with sleep, and I catch the scent of it, and it makes me ache. It makes me want her, but I can't have her here. It means something different to have someone in a bed than it does in a car. She checks her phone, and trips into the bathroom, but doesn't lock the door.

Hey, she calls through the gap, I can drive all the way back, can't I?

*

I watch her biting her lip at junctions and wonder if she ever thinks about how her life would fit twice into mine with room to spare. I wonder if she loves me, and if she does love me what that feels like to someone so young. I wonder if I was her first – that time at the far end of the industrial estate when she bled, when she held me like she was trying to crush our bodies together into one single person.

It's a fortnight before I have Ben again. I dig my appointment book out of the glove compartment and look at all those empty boxes. Lessons scrawled in smeared blue ink. The weekend circled. As messy as the house. I wind down the window and let the book tumble out, away, flapping open like a bird, loose pages spilling beneath the tyres of the lorry that follows behind. I wind the window back up. I feel good for a little while.

She misses the turning to her street, and swears under her breath. It's okay, I say. Just keep on going. She glances at me, nods. I can smell her still. Her sleeping scent like the essence of her body. Her thin arms dangle from the wheel. I take my foot off the dual controls and let her drive. Just follow the road, I say, nice and easy. Just follow the road. Keep going until I tell you to stop.

Anna Crowe

JEWELLER IN THE GALERIE ÉLECTRA, PARIS

Under glass
as though in a cabinet of curiosities
dung-beetles, crickets, mantises, bees and ants
all swarm perfectly at home
in Fabre's drawings and notebooks.

Meanwhile
a caddisfly's live, ingenious larva
is building a shelter in a tank of water;
the insect makes its calm selection
from a heap of curated materials
taking them as chance supplies them;
it tweaks fragments into place
with bristly forelegs, binding them
with sticky threads of its secreted silk
into a tubular travelling house.

This is built, not from reed straws
or the empty shells of pond-snails
(*from which it made a splendid patchwork scabbard*),
but motes of gold and flakes of turquoise
and carnelian, freshwater pearls, fashioning
in its innocence a jewelled refuge.

Note: Jean Henri Fabre, 1823–1915, is considered by many to be the father of modern entomology, pioneering the close observation of living creatures in their natural habitat. Much of his enduring popularity is due to his marvellous teaching ability and his manner of writing about the lives of insects in biographical form.

Alec Finlay

AVOCADO

she peels
and pins the stones

sets them on the sill
like a cluster

of tiny rockets
each one fuelled

by its own
glass of water

Imogen Forster

OPENCAST ARCIMBOLDO

As we approach the grey
mass the train slows to a stop.
Half the heap is missing,
what's left looks like a man's
head, haggard and unkempt.

Here are the rough cheeks,
cindery slopes whiskered
with birch scratchlings
and a thin growth of grass,
graced by a few flowers:
cranesbill, toadflax, dock.

Rough excrescences
of gorse, screes grooved
by water into deep gullies,
gravel I could work
through my fingers as if
untangling the dry hair.

The train jerks, shudders,
and through a veil of rain,
a dust-streaked cataract,
I see the heap turn skeletal,
the rim of its scoured flank
making the orbit of an eye.

My face reflected in the glass
almost exactly overlays

the mineral skull; we move
forward, leaving behind
pieces of rusty winding-gear
and one unaxled wheel.

Pippa Goldschmidt

READING MY GRANDFATHER'S GERMAN PASSPORT

I'd prefer to imagine him as a bird
at home in both sky and sea

Permitted to land at Harwich on 12 Sept 1936 on condition
that the holder does not remain in the UK longer than one
month and does not enter any employment paid or unpaid.

and able to endure the impact of diving
below the surface of the water

The condition attached to the grant of leave to land is
hereby varied so as to require that the holder does not
remain in the UK after 31 August 1937.

again and again
if I didn't know how

Permitted to land at Harwich on 5 Sept 1937 on condition
that the holder does not remain in the UK longer than
fourteen days and does not enter any employment paid
or unpaid.

some species of these birds are tracked
with devices strapped to their backs

Permitted to land at Newhaven on 6 September 1938 on
condition that the holder does not remain in the UK
after 20 January 1939.

that transmit data at ten-minute intervals
to help the Government estimate

The condition attached to the grant of leave to land is
hereby varied so as to require departure from the UK
not later than 20 May 1939.

their flight paths across the North Sea
and calculate whether they really do spend

The condition attached to the grant of leave to land is
hereby varied so as to require departure from the UK
not later than 20 May 1940.

their whole lives on the wing
never once coming to land.

Stephanie Green

CRIMSON

My mother's mouth was not strawberries
but crushed beetles, crimson with its hint of darkness,
the centre of women whispering at tea-parties.

When she entered a room, the men fell silent:
the spit of Greta Garbo, pencilled eyebrows, a bob.
Her Blitz was cartwheeling on tables at the Ritz.

On her fourth marriage, she never left the house
without putting on a face. She wore scarlet
at her brother's funeral. 'He loved me in this dress.'

The brother who'd shared their childhood, orphaned,
passed from relative to relative. After her funeral,
clearing out her dressing-table, I found,

dabbed on a tissue, her broken, faded kiss.

Lesley Harrison

EDAY, NORTH ISLES

SKAILL
the new sheep fank,
clotty turds
yellowing the turf

MILL LOCH
stirring with high cloud
grey and silver white.
a hole filled with sky

WARD HILL
all afternoon, lying
among sky coloured hills

– Mid Tooin, Keelylang
small things in the grass.

THE RED HEAD
or there, North Ron
its tempo slowed down
to two or three beats per minute.

COTT
road end.
a bay exposed to the moon.

VINQUOY
four o'clock.
the sky grows dark,
the dog bursts rabbits from the ditches.

WEST SIDE
a curlew
in a blue vein.
dead cow sinking in the turf.

NONEYHA
milk fog:
a White Sea island
silently adrift

a snowy owl
isolate, mooting
its own baltic language.

THE PIER
3am:
the turbine chirring and chirring
in new dark, in neon gleam.

Izabela Ilowska

BONES

A few days ago I saw him on the television screen. It was some evening feature programme. He was sitting in a modern studio wearing a formal jacket which seemed too tight for him. It was obvious that he didn't feel comfortable there. He had turned grey, but he still looked young. Only his eyes were different than before, many years ago, when we had been students of literature at the University of Warsaw. Somehow they seemed bigger and empty, as if they had seen too much, as if they didn't want to see anything else. I wasn't listening to what he was saying; I was just looking at him.

And I wasn't surprised to see him, after all these years, there, on television. In a way it seemed obvious. I guess I've always known that one day he and his writing would matter. Yes, we all tried to write when we were students, but only Romek knew how to do it well. His sentences were short, his words simple. Sometimes a verb was enough. Romek didn't like to play with language even though he so often admired its beauty. For him language was an instrument. It was supposed to bear witness and tell the truth, connect people. Yes, in spite of everything, Romek was an idealist. In his writing he never shocked with unnecessary brutality even when, as a young reporter for an underground newspaper, he covered the murder of two students arrested and then killed by the militia. Romek worked tirelessly. He ignored his studies, his friends and his girlfriend. Each morning he woke before dawn, drank a cup of black coffee, smoked a few cigarettes and then got on a train. He met with the striking miners in Silesia and with angry workers at the Lenin Shipyard in Gdańsk. There he listened and wrote down their stories. A few times he was arrested and questioned by the militia. But rather than daunting him, these incidents only fuelled his motivation.

With all the years that have passed, I still remember the evening when Romek and I were talking in his room in a student hostel. It was after curfew. No traffic lights, no trams or buses. The streets were dark and deserted. We were sitting on his narrow bed and drinking cheap vodka from ugly large mugs. Romek switched off the bedside lamp and put on a record. At that time he was listening to Mozart because, as he explained, he wanted to be a better person.

'I don't know why I care about her so much,' he said after a while and suddenly the room seemed even darker. 'All day she sits in her armchair and stares at some point on the wall. She doesn't speak and eats only stale bread which she washes down with cold tap water. My father can't stand this. He shouts that even in the death camp there was soup sometimes or potatoes in their skins.

'And then she looks at him. She looks at him with those dark eyes which have become so unnaturally big. They are always open, always focused on that point on the wall that seems distant and scary. She doesn't sleep. Sometimes, sitting in that old green armchair, she dozes off for a few seconds, but even then you have a feeling that she is on the alert, awake, waiting.

'Once a year she goes there, can you believe it? Once a year she rises from that shabby armchair, puts on her faded navy blue dress, gets on a bus and goes to Auschwitz. She leaves the flat very early in the morning and comes back late in the evening. Slowly and carefully she takes off her dress, hangs it on a wooden hanger, slips protective plastic over it and puts it back in the closet. She is silent and calm. Then she puts on her old green sweater, a grey woollen skirt and thick brown tights and sits in her armchair again. Her eyes are open, vigilant, unnaturally big.

'When I was younger I tried to ask her why she did this. But whenever I came near that armchair, I just couldn't do it. I couldn't even open my mouth. Now each time when I am on a train to Cracow I write down numerous questions I'd like to ask her.

It's not so difficult. But when I'm finally there I just can't force myself to go to that flat and see her. So I wander aimlessly around the streets talking to myself.

'And then I take a night train back to Warsaw. Once a month I do this, can you believe it? Once a month I go there and I never see her. I'm just as crazy as she is, I know.'

When Romek was talking about his mother, I was thinking about mine. I hadn't visited my family house for almost two years. My mother didn't sit in an old green armchair, but all day long she lay in bed. Her eyes were always closed, as if dead. During the Nazi occupation she had worked for a German family. She cleaned the small manor house, cooked and took care of two small children. When she was still healthy I tried to ask her about that time, but she said that there was nothing to say really, that the war had ended a long time ago. And then she would usually go to her bedroom, lie down on the bed and close her eyes.

Now Romek is sitting in a television studio again and talking about his new book. And I am looking at his eyes which are wide open, vigilant and frightened and wondering what they have seen.

Next day I ask my nurse to go to a nearby bookshop and buy me a copy of Romek's new book, a collection of reportages about Rwanda. A few hours later she returns and hands me a plastic bag with the bookstore's colourful logo. Quickly I look inside. The book is tiny and inconspicuous. On the cover there is a blurred black-and-white photo of a bent person. I believe it is a man, but I'm not sure. When the nurse leaves my flat in the evening I get out of bed and slowly go to the kitchen. I know that there is an old bottle of vodka in one of the cupboards. Finally I manage to find it and pour myself half a glass. Then I go to the living room which is dark and cold. I don't turn on the lamp, but I put the music on. It's Mozart, Symphony No. 41. I sit in my armchair, green and a bit uncomfortable, because it has been bought recently in one of those big new furniture stores with a funny name. I hold Romek's book on my lap, but I don't open it.

I know what I will find there. Romek wrote a book about the Rwandan genocide of 1994. Before that he had written about Cambodia, Darfur and Bosnia.

He had written about Poland too. On one of my bookshelves there is a book about martial law and its victims: workers shot during strike actions or during peaceful demonstrations and all those people who died in suspicious or mysterious circumstances. One day they left their homes and vanished into the blue. Their bodies were never found. Now all that's left is language: economical and simple. There are words which shock and hurt. They are there to testify to what really happened, even if at times it seems impossible.

The following day I finally open Romek's book. I have been given an injection of morphine, but still my entire body aches. I feel as if for the first time in my life I have full awareness of my own corporality. This is what I am, I say to myself. I am just a body, nothing more. And then I think of her again. I think about the day when she stopped walking. Just like that she refused to get out of bed. Then she stopped speaking. She didn't care for what happened to her. In a way on that large bed in the bedroom there was just her body, nothing more. Was there ever anything else inside of her? I wonder. Even if there once had been, it must have left that emaciated unhappy body long ago.

Romek writes about the Kigali Memorial Centre in Rwanda. In one section there are photographs of children. Romek stops near the photo of a little boy with a wide a smile and trusting eyes. Again his language is unemotional and simple. Some people find it beautiful while others regard it as impersonal and soulless. The photos of the children are illuminated with floodlights. In the introduction Romek explains that he went to Rwanda to learn and to listen. To listen and then to write it all down. So he pays attention to everything: he jots down every name, every detail even when, at first glance, it may seem unimportant or trivial. He manages to track down the little boy's relatives and finds out that he always asked many questions and enjoyed bedtime stories. In his notebook he writes down his name.

'Why do I tell my stories? For whom do I write?' asks Romek in the introduction of his book. But he doesn't provide any answers.

Romek had written about forensic anthropologists excavating mass graves in Bosnia in the aftermath of war. He became friends with one of them, a man, who had dug up and helped to identify hundreds of bodies. In post-war Bosnia bones were everywhere: in mass graves, but also in forests, caves, wells or in rubbish dumps. Some bones got jumbled together. It was like a jigsaw puzzle. But for this man, patient and meticulous, every bone was equally important. Sometimes he was successful and out of the heap of skeletons he was able to put a person back together.

For Romek every word is like a bone, equally important.

That night when we were sitting on his uncomfortable bed in a student hostel he told me that his mother didn't want to talk about it: about the war, about the death camp or about the child who had been taken away from her and whom she never saw again. Romek was in his teens when he found out that he had a brother. He heard about it by accident from his father who came home drunk one night. Afterwards no one ever mentioned the child. Romek never learned his brother's name.

I waited for my mother to talk to me, too. For years she lay in bed: motionless, cold, with her eyes closed. There were only bones inside of her skinny exhausted body. But those bones were silent and empty. The bones about which Romek writes refuse to be silent. They scream.

Why did they stop speaking: my mother and his? Romek still wants answers; I have given up a long time ago. He travels around the world and listens to stories about the most horrifying atrocities. Then, patiently, he pieces together the words that he hears. When my mother died, I got rid of all her diaries and letters; I got rid of every word.

A few weeks later on the radio I hear that Romek plans to go to Africa again. I'm not surprised. During the day I rarely think of him, but sometimes late at night, sitting in my new green armchair, I wonder if he still listens to Mozart.

Anita John

SOMEONE SHOUTED

Coyote! & we reined in the horses
to silence and the silent sun,
beating down. Then suddenly –

flow of sand through sagebrush
& long, dry grasses –
flow of sand lean and low
to the ground.

Those behind asked *why the wait?*
& we mouthed, *Coyote!*
as we might not speak aloud
the close proximity of bear or wolf.

Coyote kept his distance, circling round,
flowed through long, dry grasses –
a long, lean shape, lonesome,
crossing lonesome ground.

Shane Johnstone

THE WURL AS EXPERIENCIT BI SEAMUS RICHARDSON OAN THE 18TH AUGUSTE

In spite ae ma cripplin introversion an paralytic awareness ae the cliches that confront 'ower' educatit wirkin class autodidactical scrievers at each turn, descriptions ae days lit the 18th ae August, if documentit weil an pit intae willin hauns, may bi some uise tae ither cripplt cynics, fellow sufferirs ae the modirn academic sneer an introverti.

It cam as a series ae sensorie waves, o grand space an wyrd visuale wondirs, though maist wid caw thum impairment an hallucinatione. Thon wid bi the maist desirable situatione, much less, they'd label iz some kidder oan, wid luik at me thirsel as cynics, as if Ah'm neithir tellin the truth ae whit did happen, nor lyin, wi thir brows raisit taewards iz, thumsel enjoyin a wise wird tae thirsels:

'*Ach, Seamus, ayeways tryin ae bi quirky, tryin ae lose eez mun amang aw eez guid fortune, eh cannae hack it.*'

Oan wakin, fae a non-sleep, e'es partin heavy, wance, twice, the ceilin direct afore me a vast cream expanse, wi ripples alang it's bordirs in the fashione ae thae archaic Glesga architects, wee flowiry vase like ornaments faw oot an doon at parts, the pynt ae which Ah've nevvir graspt, the permanence ae architecture huvvin ayeways gied me a deep fear an dizziness. The day but, it gies a focus that helps the boady understaun that sleep isnae an option in these wyrd oors atween night n day. These first wide moments ae this day let me aware that Ah'm tae be affordit a windae ae the type Ah've bin chasin. These windaes come oan me less an less these days as Ah accept the divine circumstances affordit tae me bi the Wheel Ae Fortune, though Ah hae begun tae document thum tae the best ae ma abilitie, Ah cin pinpynt nae credible patterne or method fir summonin thum, though lack ae sleep doesnae inhibit thum as ye might expect, Ah suspect the opposite, mibbe through causin some dent in the brain's natural frantic pull taewards ego which fuels ma obsessive need fir tangible progress an study ae the languagees ae ma ancestors.

A full awareness ae each limb, in particular, ma twa feet, in the form ae a slight pull doonwards, a pull awiy fae the circular buzz in ma heid, allowis ma focus tae faw in the middle ae the boady, as Ah steps oot the bed an casts the sheets aside, sheets that the day seem sae much mair saft white an awthegithir fluffy an smashin. Ma wife stirrs wi a frown but disnae wake. Next tae wir bed is the wean's wee cot, cheap light wid that a dear freen pit thegithir, nae maistirwirk ae craftsmanship, bumpy an no parallel tae the flair but which the day fills ma usually dull an skeptical chest wi warmth, somethin that Ah cin only openly admit in the written wird.

This unexpectit burst ae emotione, causes iz tae see, no afore me, no in the ruim so tae speak, as in, in the wiy ye'd see a big orange ape sittin oan yir rug that wis therr wi-oot questione, but absolutely see, a visual web stretchin across aw generations ae ma faimly, his faimly, lit a cabinet, wi wee compartments, in each wan a scene, played oot, maistly terrible miserable events lit the potato famine, the Highland Clearances, emaciatit croftirs an teachirs beatin weans, that, in the spirit ae attemptit honestie, gie me some comfort as the roots tae the tree ae ma whale identitie, an the rage that thir injustice provokis, is as near tae comfort as the idea ae coffee that draws me oot ma scratchir. Ah allow masel tae gloriously dwell oan the unfairness ae it, this web ae terrible events, stertin fae the tap left but dottit wi a poakit in the air noo an agin, thinkin that they happent so that some divine message could be receivit bi a later decendant fir later consideratione wance meanin has bin trampelt oot the wurl bi comfort. Ah thank God in a moment ae defiance, in mind ae ma atheist pals who've nae interest in great written wirks that raise the spirit, juist oan the aff chance I'm affordit the wirds in that moment. It's near . . .

Slottit amang this displaye, every pursuit that Ah undertak frantically in ma spare time – the study o the languagees that fills up the tap ae ma heid wi stable tangible identities, an that wee windae leads tae two mair, two lenses, two whale cultures, they display masel through these lensees, the cosy intellectual comfort ae French, the melancholy blackness ae Scottis Gaelic, an awiy intae some cosmic geometric floatin darkness beyond wirds.

Ah come back, intae the ruim, the kitchen, an wir baith starvin, me an the wean. Eez screams pierced it Ah hink, ma bubble. Ah funnel a boatle ae mulk doon eez gub, the wee gannet cin open eez gullet lit a pelican, an it's gone, leavin um in that state ae content wondirment, which we baith pondir aer as soothin fatigue laps at me. Me an him, we sit doon, him oan ma gut, me wi a slice ae breed, an a coffee that Ah cannae mind makin. This junctione ae a Sunday is usually gied tae tense study ae wan ae ma obsessions, ma 'illnesseees,' as ma wife cries thum wi an empathetic smile. It'll bi cheeks clencht in attempt tae absorb some Sartre essay or face scruncht aer Ulysses, usually, but the day isnae. Somethin is in place ae the pull ae frantic learnin, wherr Ah wid gorge oan irregular verbs an think masel much advancit, take a verbal whitey tae mak ruim fir mair, cram wi clenched cheeks til ma heid is sair. In its place, this Sunday the 18th, is sweepin, airy space, ye cin near hear the calm whooshin lit the win that passees yir hoose.

Wirds swirl aroon the ruim lit wee, dare Ah uise the obvious, dandelions, an though Ah cringe at the floweryness ae that statement, Ah see thum absolutely. We sat therr surroondeed bi vision an blurry waves, an the coffee meets the breid in ma gut, before ma mind sterts wanderin in the direction ae paintin pictures ae whit the various bacteria in therr might bi wirkin oan, the wee yin's e'es, a silver that weans cin huv when gaun through optic transformation, open in that wiy that happens eftir a feed, thir wee brows furrowt, if ye luik closely ye see the wee pupils practisin tae adjust, these moments suck ye right oot yir heid, awiy fae the graspin autodidactic blitz that props up a lack ae talent an baws, sucks ye intae *their* state, fir a few moments, hauds ye therr wi thum.

A wee unhurried haun oan the shoodir, a maw touch, transferrin empathy, she's up an well restit, Ah took the night shift, Ah don't mind it. She asks me if Ah slept wi concirn oan the edge ae her voice, Ah say aye, feelin in this moment that Ah've slept a thousand year, even bypassit the need fir it. That toast smell that maks yir stomach leap oan coffee driven mornins when a tate too much acid swims in yir gut, a comfortable nausea, a marker ae ten mair minits ae the clock passin.

In ma line ae visione is her white fluffy housecoat that Ah uised tae rip it ootae but noo understaun, it trails oan the flair, her visione goes tae it tae, the cat paws at it, Ah stare at it fir atween twinty seconds an years, til she's back, she's been awiy an the space has been fillt wi shapes an colours that surroond a patch, it draws me taewards it an ma heid nods but the wean stirrs an Ah stiy upright, if Ah move therr'll bi hell tae piy.

In atween noddin aff, the wirds in various languagees begin taewards me, they swirl in a wee spiral taewards ma heid an entir ma coupon, Ah nod, nod, the weans oan ma stomach, eh stirrs again, noo she appears tae take um, Ah rise, aw the while aware ae baith legs, the hefty muscle at the back, gies a dull tug inward, Ah smile fir bein aware ae it, a gift, an though logic pulls fae the tap ae ma heid, fightin tae engulf ma boady, this exceptional day favours the boady, an as Ah rise wi the usual heid-rush Ah breech the surface an swim oot tae some plane that's right here where the edgees ae each object ae furniture is laced wi certainty.

'*Darling, Ah think ye shuid go ae bed firra bit, yir e'es ur red.*'

'*Nah nah, this day is perfect, Ah love you an Ah love the wean an Ah'm no gonnae shut it oot even though it maks me a bit uncomfortable.*'

She knows this type ae talk, Ah've a habit ae expressin each thoaght tae her, in a measurt wiy, since aboot three year ago when

Ah acceptit truly that it wisnae wan ae divers versions ae me she loved. She knows the wirkins ae ma internal life thoroughly, the wirkins that unfortunately she's stuck wi sin aw ither beins mak me deeply nervous an summon fae me a caricature ae a wirkin class Glaswegian Screiver Atheist Skeptic who maks the irritatin pynt ae spikkin the wiy eh writes, who ruins an tramples guid, fun conversatione wi Sartre, Kerouac an Joyce, who disnae follae the fitba an is middle class in aw wiys but financially an in any mattirs regardin will.

Hungir wakes iz wi a jolt. Aw WHIT! Flash ae irritation, Ah missed some ae ma windae, the wean's message wis interruptit, wan hing will claw it back.

Ah showir wi fragile optimism, Ah lucidly imagine wi vain twenty-twenty fore-hindsight ma wife's perceptione ae me as optimism gaithirs roon ma form an that the air vibrates roon wir wee bubble, the three ae iz, we'll go tae the park, we'll get coffee, an thir will be wan moment that Ah'll see it again, the windae, the haly display wi the answirs, we'll git haim an Ah'll follae it, at its end will be the end ae ma drout, Ah'll rattle it, twa, three oor, Ah feel the satisfactione that it will bring, but first, first, the weans e'es, ye huftae firget yirsel, Seamus.

Thirr's a wee cafe in Pollok Park, the coffee is weak, we sit ootside defiant in the clammy Auguste air, an it hits me, as it does, as Ah secretly suspect an hide fae masel, Hamsen, Kerouac, Joyce, great scrievers, miserable men, great trancendencie through sufferin . . . yir wife an wean, who want ye tae clambir doon fae yir ridiculous lofty heid heights an intae Pollok Park, a momentary struggle, a pop, an colour floods intae vision. She senses Ah've come back, she doesnae know how long fir, so we drink wattery coffee an say nothin, smilin.

Suzy A. Kelly

THRUM

I don't know what time it is, but the tearaways next door are squabbling again.

Rolling over, my mouth tastes like the inside of a compost bin. The metal catch on yesterday's bra nips my spine.

Soon, the whines of the potato-headed toddlers turn to outraged wails. Making a fist, I imagine breaching the plaster, bricks, and mortar to punch them square in their soft, little mouths so hard that it knocks them out of their football team bedspreads and out their bedroom window. I picture them landing on the trampoline in their back garden, and once they're trapped behind the high walls of the safety cage, I submit to the darkness for a while longer.

An hour later, the radio alarm announces a breakdown on the M77; my only route into work. So, my ablutions start with screaming into a pillow and 20mg of Citalopram to take the sharp edges off the day.

*

The rain-soaked motorway fizzes with rush hour traffic as I exit the M77. Pulling into work, aiming for the usual spot – two spaces to the left of the zebra crossing at the main entrance – a white Kia sails in ahead of me. I give a vigorous two-fingered salute, which the Kia's occupants ignore. So I reverse slowly, rev the engine, and speed forward into the next space. I catch my predator's red-faced grimace in the rear-view mirror. All my incisors are on show, ready to tear out their throats. The people in the Kia pay attention to me now with their arms outstretched, their palms up. What's my problem? What's your problem? Fucking space invaders.

A dumpy, white-haired woman in a pleather jacket chooses that moment to exit the car; all chunky thighs and tan tights. Her pastel, high-street blouse bulges under the pressure of her monstrous tits. The driver is far younger than her. The skinny adolescent – probably the daughter – is all ripped jeans with a white stripe bleached into her side-parting. They lock the Kia and hurry towards the Tesco at the opposite end of the shopping centre, obviously in a rush to snap up own-brand beans and discounted pasties.

I want Skunk-head Skinny Jeans and Mrs McSquishy Tits to trip over a bush and I imagine their chins smiling open and their blood spritzing across the wet tarmac like a Jackson Pollock number. Who do they think they are? I work here.

*

My kitten heels drum a steady click-clack across the shopping centre tiles. Cringing at my reflection in the storefronts, I check my watch and manage a curt, 'Good morning,' to the boy at the pop-up phone accessories stall. What's he got to be chirpy about? I've got knicker stains older than him.

Roll on six-thirty: clothes off, hot water, peace.

*

Young Lindsay is back in Beauty today. She's been away for the last few months. College exams I expect. She forces a smile as I cross the threshold, knowing not to speak to me before lunchtime. Especially today. That's it, blondie. Look away. Line up your perfume samples and your hairdryers. This is as good as your life gets.

I dash through Jewellery only to slow down around Childrenswear, still swallowing the chemical fog from designer perfumes. A white cotton sleepsuit in the centre display arrests me. It makes my arms feel heavy.

Just then, an anxious Ruth waves to me from Womenswear.

'Hurry up,' she mouths.

Her sharp cheekbones and tight, matronly bun accentuate the severity of her death stare.

'Coming,' I grunt, biting my cheek so as not to mention the Golden Beige foundation lines trowelled over her wrinkles.

Her red leather handbag doesn't even match her shoes. I picture strangling the woman until her wheelie-bin-green eyes pop out of her head and roll under the sales counter. Then I'd say, 'Ruth, sweetie, for a personal shopper, your fashion sense is gash.'

*

Pre-consultation checks are complete and I collate clothes from across the different designers: all the velvet, cotton, lambswool, and lace needed for a new Autumnal wardrobe. This morning, it's for the benefit of a middle-aged pregnant divorcee called Carol, and a young widow called Dawn. There could be commission on Christmas partywear for me, if I steer them right.

The women drink the complimentary fake wine as I teach them about the most stylish cuts and fabrics for them. For Carol, it's about how to flatter her curves and, for Dawn, it's about how to amplify her assets.

'Give this a try,' I say to Carol, presenting her with a plus-sized, satin dress. 'You'll see its matching three-quarter-length coat frames you perfectly . . . now reduced to £175 . . .'

'What about this?' I tell Dawn. 'Cranberry, polyester jumpsuit. Contrasting cap sleeves. You can match it with a new pair of strappy sandals for that extra height . . .'

Each woman poses in the full-length mirrors before rejecting my art with a flustered, 'Aye, hen, but it's just no me.'

Ungrateful fucks.

*

Lunch time: my usual sandwiches in the car along with 20mg of Propranolol to ease the hammering in my chest.

I could walk the long way back to the shop entrance – past Gifts & Toys – or I could brave it and pass Childrenswear again. That would mean facing Dev, who knows what today is.

'Lighten up,' he'll say.

And I'll say, 'Watch me lighten your face by ripping off your fucking ears and wearing them as a necklace.'

Tightening my fists, I stride past the baby shoes and designer bibs with idiotic statements like 'Mummy's Little Princess' printed on them. But they're not going to beat me, not this year. But soon, the vinyl walkway is in the distance and I'm weaving between the racks until that damned sleepsuit is there in front of me. Staring at its empty, fur-lined feet, I stroke the yellow chick on its chest. 'Just Hatched', it reads underneath. Like a passenger in my own brain, I snatch the sleepsuit from its hanger and tuck it into my blouse.

I see Dev at the store entrance and stall. He's boring Lindsay again as she stands out front wafting cardboard perfume samples at the customers. He's fooling himself. As if she'd be interested in his golf handicap or his bank account.

Their mouths open into wide 'O's as I speed towards the security barriers and set off the alarms.

Click-clacking my way out of the shopping centre, I stare down every pedestrian in my path and imagine their heads exploding like fireworks in single and multiple illuminated bursts. Back in the car, I break.

*

Dev taps the window. I'm still nursing the stolen sleepsuit over my shoulder.

'Hannah, let me in . . .'

There's no sharpness, just warm resignation in his voice, which is worse. If he'd shouted, got my back up . . .

I tap off the central locking.

'Please don't . . .' I cry, expecting some kind of barb from him.

But he installs himself in the front passenger seat. There's no bad jokes from him. No snippy remarks. Just the perfect gift, silence. There's nothing left for us to argue about or blame each other for.

It takes a while, but my whole body unclenches. Dev reaches out then and guides my head onto his shoulder, one last time.

'I feel it too,' he says, squeezing my hand.

At the tenderness, I bury my nose in the sleepsuit and imagine it swelling with kicking, breathing flesh. A silent howl begins inside my head.

'Dev, maybe if I didn't insist on having sex that night . . . maybe . . . we were still in the first trimester for fuck sake . . . I should have known . . .'

He pulls his hand back.

'We've been over this, Hannah,' he sighs, 'so many times. It's not your fault.'

*

I watch Dev slope towards the 'Staff Only' area with the sleepsuit protruding from his trouser pocket. He promised to sneak it back onto its little hanger. It'll be like it never happened.

'Back shortly,' he says in his managerial way, as if we'd never been intimate, never once Christened the sofa in his office.

No doubt he'll be scrubbing my mascara off the baby clothes in the gents while he curses me for my 'drama'.

*

'Better get a move on,' says Ruth on my return to Womenswear. 'Your last appointment is—'

'Thanks,' I say, cutting her off.

'I covered the others,' she snaps, 'if you feel like thanking me?'

I feel like kicking her passive-aggressive head into the display cabinets and imagine a thousand shards of streak-free glass slicing her botoxed face open.

'What are you smiling at?' says Ruth.

'Nothing.'

And here it comes:

'Oh, get over your bloody self,' she says, stamping down cardboard boxes for recycling. 'We're women. We've all had . . . something.'

My head feels like it's stuffed with fibreglass.

'Fuck you,' I explode.

*

Sounds are powerful. One moment I'm in the present with the client, then one clash and clink of metal curtain rings later, and I'm not here. My mouth makes professional introductions to the cross-legged woman on the dark purple chaise longue, but my head is lost.

On opening the dressing room curtain, I'm back in the hospital. It's visiting hour. On standing up to use the commode, something inside me lets go. There's this hard, wet, smacking noise, like paint hitting the pavement. An angry-red mass drops onto the lino. Nurses haul the bedside curtains closed behind them, uttering soothing, but well-practiced words. I remember soft pats on my back. There's encouragement to lie down and assurances that everything will be fine.

'Common in first-time pregnancies,' they say.

The memory hits and I breathe into it until it passes, digging my nails into my palms until the waves subside.

*

'Night,' says Lindsay on my way out.

She gives me a look, willing me to hang back.

'You probably heard they took the left ovary in the op,' she whispers.

Department stores are usually like small villages, but I've been left out of this particular loop.

'Oh,' I say, a little winded. 'Nobody said . . .'

'That's why I was off for so long.'

'Ah.'

'I thought you'd understand?'

'Err, yes. Sorry,' I mumble, and then I'm squeezing her arm a little, one could-have-been-mum to the other.

She returns the act of solidarity by pulling her shirt sleeve up to reveal a small tattoo on her wrist. It's a loop of pink ribbon that changes colour halfway through into a soft powder-blue. The tag below it reads 'Angel'. I want to grab a wire brush and scrub that cursive lettering off until her skin dissolves. But I get it. I get her.

'Take care,' I say, this time meaning it.

Ingrid Leonard

MAESHOWE – I

Some slock they must hiv hin on them,
haevan man-shorn rock fae quarry tae dig,
their own hand's deueen hewn intae the face o it.
A hunder thoosand hoors takan water fae the burn
at mid-morning, tae the soond o whaups and stone-chats
afore the setting o fower dolmen an a corbelling
o sand and feldspar till a domed ceiling they hid,
harled wi stone and clay fae the lochside.
Their lives were short; too many corpse-shells
o bairns, mithers and menfolk set tae rot in voar
an too many left tae mind them, so they built
a womb on the plain whaur the sunset shone
at the turn o the year and to it they carried bones
o their loved ones, tae warm in midwinter's spark.

slock: quench
hiv hin: have had
deueen: doing
whaup: curlew
stone-chat: wheatear
fower: four
hid: had
voar: spring

MAESHOWE – II

By the light of the waxing moon
the bone-cleaners worked, burrowing
through earth left alone for a year.
Night had stretched to full volume,
singing dominion over eye and ear;
a forkie-tail quivered under stone.
The dead must remain in their darkness
until bathed and placed in new year's light.
The living lit fires, soused skull and rib
in saltwater scuttle till the design
of their kin gleamed bare and white,
licked and dried by firelight and carried
in sweat and song to the earth's clean womb
to be blessed by a sun gaining strength.

Shona McCombes

AMONG THE PIGEONS

The cats are outside again, wailing their dark ungodly wails from somewhere on the hills. It frenzies him gently: a slow building pressure in the chest, a rising intensity of sensation. Lying flat on his back, he tries to block it out by concentrating on the hard knot of metal that lies heavy in the drawer, running his mind across its curves and edges, its elegant internal machinery, the noises he could wring from it. He twitches. No use, not at this time; he does not know where they are. The echoes ricochet off rock and pine, cloaking their origin in the clamour. He knows what they are doing. His dreams are infested.

The morning is still and damp. In his small neglected garden, a scattering of pots wither on unkempt grass, things growing that were not put there but have taken the initiative to make space for themselves. By the door a basket hangs, unplanted. Glancing out as he slices skin from flesh, he sees a bird has settled there. She turns her head a fraction, meets his eye. A plump calm familiar thing, slate-grey; the kind of rounded body that looks like it would be satisfying to cup between the hands, firm and tender. He steps towards the hob, and at the sudden movement a ripple passes through her feathers, an agitation, then stillness again. Waiting for the oil to heat he regards her, regarding him. The meat hisses as it hits the pan.

After eating he goes out into the fine sheet of rain that hangs over the land, endless, and walks. He scans ceaselessly among the trees, glancing occasionally towards the slivers of visible sky. It is quiet and still and then a flurry of small birds sends drops of moisture spinning from the leaves, branches bouncing softly with the motion of sudden abandonment. Then it is quiet again, and he keeps walking and looking, looking and walking.

He takes the usual routes, and some new ones. At certain moments he pauses, crouches; the traps remain empty.

After some hours, finally, on the long curve of path that leads back to his house, down in the damp green foliage, there is something: a familiar kind of rustle, a flash of yellow eye. He is slow and careful. Its nearness does not bode well for its genealogy; the real ones keep their distance. They were here before the land was settled, a long time before, and they keep to the wilder places, out far past where the roads abruptly finish and the paths gradually vanish, in the fragments of a deep past where their sovereignty might not yet be usurped. The nearer one gets, the further it is likely to be from what he is searching for. Still, he allows himself to harbour a small and unarticulated hope. Sometimes they stray.

But he runs his gaze over the coat, the tail, the skull, the stance, and subdues that hope for another day. Some of the ones he meets are close imitations. The furtive offspring of those dark ungodly unions, markings close enough to provoke a moment of hesitation – only off somehow, uncanny, like a picture sketched from memory and missing some small crucial feature. This one, though, is nothing. Too frayed and frightened to be a pet, so a feral thing, out on its endless desperate hunt. It is frozen there in the undergrowth, staring, and he looks it in the eye as the noise moves through him, reverberating from the hand to the heart, the groin, the stomach. It is important to him, this principle: he always looks them in the eye. It is a matter of respect.

When he arrives back home, the bag heavy in his hand, he pauses by the hanging basket. The pigeon is not there, but she has nested, and two white eggs sit fragile and exposed.

*

On the television they are in Edinburgh, talking to a woman who works for the zoo. The panda, she says, is in her brief window of fertility, and they are optimistic about the possibility of pregnancy.

Pandas in captivity, she says, are notorious for their reluctance to mate, but there are new reproductive technologies, new breeding techniques. The interviewer says something trite and tedious – something about the wonders of science, something about a new member of the Scottish–Chinese family. He twitches. Every year this endless fuss over an animal that should have been left to its slow death long ago. An evolutionary dead end; a lethargic, bloated species, lacking in drive and dignity. So much money and such a dreadful saturation of images, so many eyes transfixed and heartstrings pulled, as if this – he watches them, lolling among the carefully arranged greenery behind a sheet of glass covered in sticky human fingerprints – as if this had anything to do with nature. Importing impotence on a plane and not a whisper for the filth going on outside. He changes the channel. Another boat has gone down in the Mediterranean. He turns the television off.

While he slices flesh from bone he thinks, as he often does, about Martha. The last of the passenger pigeons, 1914, dead with the rest of them that year. He has never been to America, but he has read a lot about its flora and fauna, its geological fault lines, its weather systems. The human parts of it he finds distasteful, a crude synthetic culture, but under it all still some vestige of majesty. He would have liked to be alive in the years when it was all new and unimagined, untrammelled, and three billion passenger pigeons shrieking across the skies like a storm.

Martha, for her part, never made it to the sky. She lived and died in a zoo, barren and weak, and today she lives on in a glass case, a carcass forced to embody a history it never knew. He found a website, once, with a three-dimensional image of her remains, spinning endlessly, so that you can see the last of the passenger pigeons from any angle, from anywhere in the world, at any time. He has read a lot about extinction. In recent writing, animals like Martha have begun to be referred to as *endlings*. He finds it a feeble word, and strange in the plural. Not an accumulation of things alike, but a disjunction: a collection of creatures defined by their difference, by the unbridgeable gulf between them. There were other contenders for the honour of naming this phenomenon: *relict*, a solemn nod to the profundity of time; *terminarch*, more regal and dignified. It does not surprise him, in this saccharine age, that the soft childishness of *endling* won out. The very act of naming it, besides, strikes him as vaguely insulting. An endling is alone is this world, more utterly alone than any human being could ever hope to be, and in exchange for that solitude it gets the paltry token of an identity. He glances at the bird in the basket, a commonplace creature, and in a sudden gesture of generosity or derision he decides to name her for that distant, distinguished relative. Martha.

But at least there is a finality to it all, a definitiveness, a date and time of death; his mind turns back, as the meat hisses in the pan, to the day's work. There will be no endling among the Scottish wildcats – no relict, no terminarch. They say there are less than a hundred of them left, the pure ones; some say there are less than a dozen. They are the last real predators on these isles, ferocious and reclusive, and they are being allowed to disappear into the recesses of memory like everything else that was ever worth a damn. The wildcat is destroying itself not by impotence or inactivity but by a perverse excess of virility. The wildcat will not stay to its own kind; it intermingles with those frightened half-human things, and with each ungodly union it waters down its wildness until nothing is left untouched. There are hundreds of thousands of them, the cats we brought with us across the sea, tarnished by breeding and warmth but impossible to contain, multiplying and seducing and everywhere. And so the last of the Scottish wildcats will be an indeterminate creature, impossible to pin down to a single body. The last of the Scottish wildcats is an idea that flows through the blood of every housecat he hears shriek in the night, every feral beast he meets out there in the forest, everything that affects a wildness not proper to its kind. With each new litter the gene pool degenerates, and the wild becomes a little weaker, a little less fierce and proud and reticent. It is a slow and anguished extinction, humiliating: not the bang of a death, decisive and final, but the whimper of a feral labour that marks the end of the line. Though he has never met one in the flesh, he feels this degradation with a strange intimacy, as if it were his own. At times it is too much to bear. But he does what he can.

He eats, that night, with a certain satisfaction.

*

After a time the eggs hatch. He looks down upon them while Martha is out collecting worms. They are grotesque, unfamiliar things, prehistoric almost, dark and spiny. They do not resemble the adults of their kind.

Many days pass without encounter. The traps are empty still, the hills darkened and deserted; he drives into the village to buy his meat. Outside the shop, a pram has been left unattended, a small and fragile body left exposed. He pauses a moment and regards it, regarding him. Babies are obscure things; he has never had the urge to produce one, though he understands that it is what drives other urges, the ones he can neither evade nor fulfil. The child's face flickers and contorts as it holds his gaze, in delight or discomfort. It is an animal yet to enter the world of meaning, but draped already in the trappings of humanity, unable to escape the path on which it has been set. It is for the best, he thinks, that his genes remain locked in this decaying body. He does not know what he might do confronted with his own gaze.

The mother appears, startles slightly at him standing there. Her hair is bright and harsh, a pigment not found in any plant, clashing violently with the grey that hangs in the air, clattering into the atmosphere and disrupting its precarious equilibrium. As she grips the pram she ventures a smile. Not from around here.

He turns without meeting her eye, and wraps up his disgust to savour later, in privacy.

The cats have been quiet these last days. Maybe it is the storms and the rain, which have been more relentless than usual. They will be keeping to the dark sheltered places. The ones that are closer to domesticity, able to mask their feral habits – some only a generation or less from the cosseted life of the pet – will be creeping quietly into gardens, sidling up to back doors, sliding into cat flaps. Children will delight and plead; adults will indulge, put down food, allow themselves to be seduced into sharing their warm spaces. They are skilled manipulators, moving from home to forest, forest to home, not fully belonging to either but able to put on the customs of both. Everywhere in the world the same story: an epidemic.

The pure wildcats do not approach human habitation. They have the dignity to know their proper place.

*

On Wednesdays he drinks in the village pub. Only on Wednesdays: by Friday the place is teeming with daytrippers and bus tours, an unbearable grating chaos of voices, and on Mondays and Tuesdays it is closed. He seldom speaks to anyone. There was a time when he thought he wanted one of the bartenders – a small, sturdy woman with a local accent and a sharp face that seems always to be tinged with something between repulsion and resignation. There was a time when he thought they might be the same, she and him, and once or twice he forced himself to say something more after she had given him his beer and his change. But every time she started to speak something shifted in her face; the dark sharp look would drop away as they traded banalities. Since then he has seen her after shifts, sitting at the bar with groups of friends or colleagues, face wide open and laughing like the rest of them, and he has realised that the look was a fantasy, a trick of skin and lighting, signifying nothing: she is just another part of the world, moving through it in contented ignorance. These infatuations, he knows, are imprudent and childish. Every time one grips him he is bathed in his own contempt.

He used to write a lot of letters. To politicians and charities and newspapers; at that time he believed that he could save them by conventional means. He volunteered, for a time, with the government-run conservation programme, and then for a longer time with another organisation that had different ideas. Both, in the end, turned out to be timid and bloodless, unable to stomach the dirty work. Fixated on captive breeding and expensive genetic technologies, on laborious neutering programmes, on gentle persuasion of a disinterested public. With age he has come to understand that minds are not for changing, that people are stupid and selfish creatures who do not understand what they are allowing to happen. They are soft and sentimental, and steeped in this absurd modern aversion to any kind of sacrifice. Democracy will never consent to anything as vulgar as eradication, and the wildcat will not survive anything less. He has not ceased to write, though he knows that all the words he releases into the internet's void are impotent; it is a leftover urge that he cannot repress. There is some small comfort in the occasional encounter with others like him, the handful that remain, scattered about the country – men who still value history and heritage, who have respect for nature's proper domain. But knowledge is not enough. To get things done he has only himself to rely upon.

*

He is out at dawn the day he comes across the deer. It is a clear day after weeks of rain and the hills are in motion, shadowed with passing clouds and patches of gold. Rounding the hillside at the point where the forest opens out into an expanse of grass, far out beyond the village where walkers rarely stray, it rises suddenly into his line of vision, and it takes his eyes a moment to register what he is looking at. A slumped shape, a cage of brittle bones, and missing the part that would make it cohere into something recognisable: it is a body without a head. There are more of them, he begins to realise, scattered across the hillside; he walks among them slowly. The remains of the cull, left for picking clean by birds or rotting slowly back into soil. Some of them are partial, some near-intact, and in this state they seem somehow more individual than they ever were in the homogenous herd of the living. Each is marked out by its state of decay, by which parts are missing and which still attached, by the precise and irreducible sprawl of its limbs where it has fallen. He looks at them for a long time. He has seen his share of dead animals, but never this many all at once, never so large. It sends tremors through him.

When he arrives home that day he looks, as he always does, to Martha's basket and something is there that should not be there: poised on the wall above, gazing down intently, moving its hind in preparation to pounce. Its coat blooms with dark blurred rosettes on rusted fur; it is long and lithe and muscular, wild in a foreign way, not of the forest but the jungle – a body bred for predatory beauty, generations of carefully selected genes culminating in this, a pastiche of its exotic ancestors. It senses his movement and flicks the gaze in his direction, freezes, legs tense with kinetic energy on the verge of release. He twitches, and feels it overcome him – a strange possessive sensation, like jealousy or love – and takes out the gun. Never this close to home before. The noise blooms over his house. The birds startle and shuffle restlessly in their nest, half-formed feathers fluffing out in fear.

He realises immediately the stupidity of it. The limp body is collared with a band of embossed leather, its coat bright and luxurious. They are expensive things, not taken lightly. He carries it quickly inside.

The posters that will soon appear on trees and lampposts, the suspicious glances and accusatory questions – he does not know it yet, but they will be overshadowed and pushed to the fringes of concern by those deer on the hillside, the outrage they will ignite when someone else finds them. Too many of them, too many all at once, too many left out like that: an obscenity. A cull must be a quiet thing, if it is to survive. It will burn for weeks, this outrage; it will be in headlines about massacres and letters to editors, online screeds and carefully worded statements. And among all of this the expensive exotic cat will melt away and be forgotten. Her owner will replace the posters, petition the neighbours, ache for vengeance, but none will be drawn into the drama. There is only so much death that people can hold onto at once, only so many reserves of feeling they can draw upon. Something is always sacrificed.

*

Martha is increasingly absent; the chicks are nearly ready to fly. As he slices skin from flesh he thinks about them. It has been interesting to watch their development, but as they grow to resemble pigeons they become saturated with the significance of their species. There are enough pigeons in the world. They carpet the floors of every city in Europe; they do not belong to anywhere. Like the cats they will not stop multiplying and infiltrating, begging and stealing, carrying in their bodies the seeds of disease and destruction. As the meat hisses in the pan, he opens the back door, looks down upon them. When he leans in to look more closely, the larger of the two rears up, puffing its chest and spreading its half-grown wings as far as they will go – a small defiant gesture, a territorial warning, a proud assertion of its newly known existence. He smiles softly and reaches in. Never with bare hands before; it will be a new sensation.

Neil McCrindle

ON THE CUP

Down-crouched by the bridge, steam wisping off sodden sleeping bag in the early sunshine, Ally Coulter was shivering. A dented Starbucks cup at a tilt on the cobbles held three pennies. Grimy fingers teased scraps from a gutter dout into a crumpled Rizla and he carefully stuck it behind his ear.

Nae smokin oan the joab Ally. Lassies dinnae like it these days.

Heels clicked. Heads up.

—Ten pee furra cup o tea hen?—

If the woman heard him she didn't show it. Bustling past, sipping at a shining tube, wreathed in vapour. White shells poured music into her ears. Ally's cup was unbothered.

Down the street a dumpy, headscarfed woman eased onto her knees with a grunt. Folded her hands in supplication. Eyes followed the clenched faces of the morning office stream with mute reproach.

Clever, hen.

Ally raised his voice to a hoarse shout.

—HAW BURKA HEID, BUILDERS KNEEPADS THREE NINETY-NINE IN B&Q—

He gave a grin and a thumbs up and the woman's eyes flicked towards him. A clattering cough followed the sudden intake of chill. Ally choked —Ten pee furra cup o tea pal?— but the man had slipped past, nacreous trainers under the solemn pinstripe, leather briefcase swaying heavily. Opportunity missed.

Gone afore ye know it Ally boy. Eyes front. Yer oan the cup.

A paper scrap fluttered and lifted in the road, whirled by passing cars. Ally's gaze was fixed on it. Forehead skin moved as if pushed by an invisible finger. Sometimes he would say a word out loud, a whole sentence of an internal narrative.

—Ah should get a dug—

He looked around as if someone had whispered the thought into his ear and run away.

A key. Da's back.

—A fucken dug—

Ally's shoulders lifted and tightened.

—Ye cannae even look efter yersel. Whit can YOU gie a dug? Cold nights, nae basket, goat tae feed it. Ye dinnae want tae care fur onyhin, cannae care fur onyhin, cannae care fur yersel an if ye cannae care . . . cannae care—

—Summay they other guys huv goat dugs— Ally's voice was a petulant mutter —Marine Larry. His heid's that fucked up he needs a pal that isnae a human. Ah wid like a pal. No jist folk I huvtae hide ma stuff an masel from—

Laughter. Eyewis was a heartless cunt.

—You anna dug—

The voice was coarse and gloating.

—Stoap bein a fucken fanny—

*

—Ten pee furra cup o tea pal?—

Breeze snatched at the rollup, sparks curling around Ally's cupped hand. He yawned long and deep. Fiercely rubbed his bleary eyes.

Fucken sloggin last night man. Jist gettin tae sleep, an it starts pishin. Wisnae long likes, but heavy an wet. Seeps into yer bag, sucks away the heat. A wee smirr could go on fur oors, jist settles an sticks an yer okay, an if it's rainin steady a bit o shelter can keep that aff. But howlin wet like last night man, splashin ye, drenchin ye, that doonpipe overflow was comin aff the wa at me like bombs – that's the wettest of aw.

A line appeared between his eyebrows.

—Funny tae hink o rain bein different kinds ay wet, eh—

Eyes suddenly and silently filled with tears. He knuckled them away.

Greetin a lot these days, Ally. Onybiddy wid hink ye werenae happy. Comes an goes like. An only fur a wee bit.

—Only fucken wee poofy cunts greet—

Ally tried not to think of the stony eye, glittering red with alcohol, and shuddered.

—An ah'm lookin at a fucken wee poofy CUNT—

*

—Ten pee furra cup o tea hen?—

Ally was sullenly observing Burka Heid from the corner of his eye.

That's twice she's had folk talkin tae her. Look at they posh auld bints slappin on the sympathetic face. Away an eat yer fucken pah-stah, ya muppets.

He glared at Burka Heid's latest benefactor. Layered sensible clothes. Long grey hair. She stood up and walked away briskly. Behind her Burka Heid whipped coins out of the cup and into her voluminous skirt.

Must hae knees like ma Grandpa's bools.

Heaving himself up, Ally wandered over. The woman eyed his approach warily.

—Haw hen, wherr ye fae? Dae ye go tae kneelin school therr?—

Black eyes flickered over Ally's matted silvering hair. Fingernails black crescents of dirt. Grime in every pore. She said nothing. Her eyes dropped and she resumed her vigil.

Fucken suit yersel hen.

Rejected, Ally slumped down against the wall, felt his stained and battered sleeping bag.

Still damp.

—Here son—

Ally squinted into the sun. A hand held a Greggs sandwich pack.

—Cheers pal. Got ten pee furra cup o tea anaw?—

But his question bounced off a retreating back. Mangling

the cardboard and scooping out a sandwich, Ally chewed determinedly. Patchy stubble swept up flecks of cheese and bread. After every mouthful he probed with his finger at a back tooth.

—Fucken teeth man—

Nae yis to ony cunt. They're jist fur choppin up yir food, man. Why do they huvtae feel onyhin?

Ally crumpled the packet and dropped it.

—Litter!— A frown from under a passing flat cap.

Ally was suddenly belligerent, jaw jutting.

—Aye, that's whit ah am tae you, jist litter pal, trash oan the street . . . sweep me away pal, sweep me away!—

Flat Cap gave a snort. A hand flapped dismissively.

*

—Ten pee furra cup o tea hen?—

A woman with an armful of books. A rueful 'sorry, I couldn't possibly get my purse out' moue. Ally gazed after her.

Books, man. Too much information. How dae they cunts keep aw that stuff in their heids?

His gaze skated away.

Jimmy doon at the Cross. Likes tae read that boy. Reads oan the joab. Gie's him somehin tae dae like. Folk even gie him books. It's a lonely life this. Empty an chilly. Ye dinnae often see mair than wan guy beggin at a time but if you've goat a book, then you dinnae need someone tae talk tae, eh. But then ah'm no much o a reader.

*

—Ten pee furra cuppa tea?—

The pedestrian flow began to pick up. Lunchtime. An intermittent coin rattled Ally's cup. He nodded and grinned.

Polite noo Ally. Thank ye Sur. Thank ye Madam. Make sure ye take oot maist o it or folk hink yer wan o they beggars in the papers, makes a hunner poun a day.

He grimaced.

Ye hink beggars dinnae read the papers but ah ken yer pish. Some cunt pits oan auld claes an sits oan a corner wi his hon oot. Then he's back tae his warm hoose an eats his fucken hoo-mus an writes in his paper WORKSHY COIN IT IN. Daily Mail's guid fur stuffin yer sleepin bag wi though, plenty o it

*

—Ten pee furra cuppa tea neebor?—

Burka Heid was shovelling more coins into her drab skirt. Ally looked perplexed.

How's she daein it man?

He fixed a strolling tourist couple with a misshapen eye and bellowed.

—Over here visitors tae bonnie Scotland an meet a Scottish beggar, but no a proud one. A true flower o Scotland, a weed atween the cobbles. Ten pee furra cup o tea?—

The woman stopped and turned. Glanced coolly at Ally.

—Wait Pete. I gotta get this—

American. Get yer dollars oot hen.

She bent down. Ally leaned forward and exposed furred brown teeth in a wide smile. The woman swiftly raised a camera and adjusted a fat lens.

That's me therr.

For a second Ally stared at his reflected self, eyes manic, hair wild.

Three rapid snaps. The woman dropped a coin in his cup and pulled a piece of paper from the pocket of her jacket.

—You know, if you need help, with an addiction, you could look at this—

Paper was pushed into his cup. She stood up and walked back to her companion who was idly gazing at the granite tracery of the buildings.

—Hey Pete, remember that guy in Oaxaca? With the elephantiasis?—

They strolled on.

Puzzled, Ally pulled the paper out of the cup with two fingers. A flyer. A tanned, grinning man in a pastel shirt held hands with an equally ecstatic woman in a pink jumper. Their message read: 'We loved drink more than Jesus – until we let him into our lives.' Ally's head jerked up. With an aggrieved tone he roared in their wake.

—AH DINNAE DRINK AN AH DINNAE DAE DRUGS—

He peevishly glared at the retreating backs. Brought the flyer up to his eyes. Studied the man's straight white teeth, the hair with a slight sheen, and snorted.

Cunt looks like he's fucken polished.

Burka Heid had a man with her now. Round mustard Puffa jacket emphasising the skinniness of his legs. Fists rammed into the front pockets. Black shapeless trousers. Hems in strands around the heels of silver-buckled scuffed shoes. Burka Heid said a couple of words. Her eyes rolled sorrowfully at Ally.

The man sidled over. Pebble eyes studied the meagre copper in the Starbucks cup. Fixed on Ally's face. Stubbled, bruised, bleary. No threat.

—Why you talk her?—

The man's pockmarked chin jutted towards Burka Heid.

Ally's head jerked left. He looked away for a long time, as if trying to identify a distant pedestrian. The man bent down. Dropped a coin into Ally's cup and hissed.

—Fuck off you now—

Ally squinted at Burka Heid's minder. He dropped his head and rubbed his chin.

—Tell you whit, mate. Me fuck off? ME FUCK OFF? Whit aboot you pal? Ah'm fucken Scottish me!—

A scab-knuckled hand slapped at his chest.

—Ah live here! Ah wis born in this city an ah'll die here! Might be in an alley like but it'll be an alley ah've kent aw ma life. So ye ken where you an fucken Burka Baws ower therr can go—

Ally's rant was attracting stares. A teenager started filming on his phone. Burka Heid's minder stared impassively at a fleck of spit on his sleeve. Turning his back on Ally, he looked with great interest at the façade over the road. Burka Heid slowly raised herself with the aid of the bin and a groan and wandered off with a rolling gait. Curious bystanders now found their attention being dragged away and headed off elsewhere.

Burka Heid's minder scanned the faces left. No one who had been interested in them still was. He farted loudly and grunted. Then his foot jerked backwards. A short, sharp kick. The leather heel cracked into Ally's shin.

Ally crumpled, gasping.

As he lay prone, Burka Heid scurried round the corner. Ally jerked upright, face purple with pain and rage.

—FUCKEN GYPSY CUNT, YA FUCKEN—

But the minder was nowhere in sight. Ally fell back, rolled onto his side. Clutched at the agony with both hands, eyes screwed shut. He began to sob.

Ye want a dug? This is whit it's like to be a dug. Folk kick ye if they feel like it. Ah'm a dug to be kicked. Lower than a dug.

—A fucken greetin wee poofy cunt, so ye ur—

Ally rubbed his eyes. Dragged a sleeve across his nose, leaving a silver trail. Nobody had stopped to help or ask after him.

A greetin tramp rollin aboot oan the pavement? Aye, right.

He rolled up his trouser leg, inspected his grey shin. A raised weal looked angry.

—Hi Ally, how ye doin the day honey, ah says, how ye doin. Whit's up wi ye, eh, whit's up wi ye?—

Mary from the shelter outreach team bending over him.

That look they folk aye huv, sortay sorry like, an the kind of sorry ah dinnae need. Ah jist want ten pee o sorry. Hert in the right place Mary, but a pain in the erse at times, aye on at ye aboot lookin efter yersel. An she does that singin hing when she talks.

'Goat tae get oan myyy way – aaayy'. Like that. She repeats hersel an aw. Pure rips yer knittin.

*

Ally squinted up, rolled down the leg of his jeans.

—Ye awright Ally? Ah says, ur ye awright?—

Ally grunted. —Aye, no bad. Signin a big book deal later the day. Life on the mean streets of the Festival city. Goin fur ma lunch at the Scran an Scallie—

Mary's eyes crinkled.

—That's great, Ally. Let us know when it's oot an ah'll get ye tae sign it—

Her voice rose to a warble.

—Ah'll ken a famous aw-therrrrrr—

Ally grunted again.

—Aye, wan o ma many talents. I couldae turnt ma hon tae onyhin like. But ah nivir—

—Noo, Ally, listen tae us, ah says, listen tae us—

Time for Mary to get down to business.

—Noo, this is important, ur ye still takin yer medication? Cos we huvnae seen ye at the shelter furra while, ye've no been therr furra while—

—Naw. Someone stole it. An ah dinnae huv time tae get doon tae the centre. Busy, busy, ivry day, likes—

—Aye, well. Mind o Doctor Hanna at the centre? He wis askin efter ye. I saw him the day an he says yer medication must hae run oot by noo. An ye've got tae come in, cos he cannae write ye a prescription if he doesnae see ye. Ken whit ah mean? If he doesnae see ye, ye cannae huv a new prescription—

Ally studied Mary's face.

Mary's awright but they pit that much pressure oan ye doon the shelter. Come intae the warm, get ye a bed, get ye a wash, get ye a room, you're no gettin ony yunger. They jist dinnae unnerstaun, eh – sooner or later ah'm gonnae fuck up with somehin. Ah can jist aboot look efter masel oot here, but once they start heapin they hings on ye, bills, benefits, neebors . . . It's no nice places they pit ye in. Bad folk aroon ye. Knockin oan the door, offerin ye gear or jist pushin past ye an takin whit ye've goat an laughin in yer face. Been therr done that, widdae had the t-shirt but it goat nicked. If ye cannae cope then scratchin a livin is aw ye need. A few fags an some food, sleepin bag an that's you like, day to day. Guid enough fur they Neandery-tals an cave folk. Live today, fur tomorrow a lion eats ye.

—Well, if yer okay Ally ah'm away then, ah says, ah'm away—

Another concerned look.

—Mind whit ah says about Dr Hanna. Ah says, mind whit ah says—

*

The wind was turning chilly. Ally slowly crushed still damp folds of sleeping bag into a Sainsbury's carrier.

He sang to himself.

—Another day, another dollar, Ally my boooooy—

Jeez, noo Mary's goat me daein it anaw. Whit we goat?

A sticky handful of coins. Lips moved as he counted.

£14.71, whit's that, about a poun fifty an hour. No quite the livin wage but it'll dae.

Ally stood up, stretched.

Time tae away up an see the Sikhs at North Bridge. Guid boys like, haunin oot grub wi their turbans an gold Rolexes. Fucken great scran fae the Sikhs. Curry an rice an that. Nivir used tae huv curry when ah wis growin up. Square sausage wi ivry meal, that's whit we had. They even gie ye coffee fae Starbucks but I nivir drink it. Ye dinnae wantae be awake aw night when yer lyin in a skip.

In the river rushes, a heron stood immobile. Ally gazed entranced from the bridge.

—See that, eh?— Grinned at passers-by. —Ducks an aw, look—

A duck with a brood of ducklings paddled past the reeds. The heron stabbed. A chirruping duckling dangled from its beak.

Ally's mouth opened in horror. The frantic mother cackled in circles. The heron dunked the duckling in the river and bolted at the wet bundle. Legs kicking at the leering mouth.

A single tear formed in Ally's eye.

Dinnae . . . aw dinnae . . .

Laughter. A key in the lock.

—C'mere poofy cunt—

With a last jerking gulp, the duckling disappeared. The heron spread its wings. Lumbered into the air. Glided away over the red waters.

Cruel eye.

Ally's face creased.

Fucken cruel eye.

Stuart Macdonald

WHITE WIND TURBINE, HARTHILL

Like an Isle of Man ballet dancer it glides like a famous
Dutch footballer turning on a sixpence like hands
conducting a whispering symphony like a waxed lyric
rolling off the tongue like another ice cold Tennents sliding
down the throat like the talking of the trees like an
albatross soaring across the deep like turning water into
wine like a sea star crucifixion like a ticking clock on exile's
wall like a sleepwalking spider like radio silence like a
memorial for the curlew like *Strangers on the Shore* on
white vinyl like taking the ferry or crossing bridges like
snowflakes that swirl at Christmas like que sera sera
whatever will be will be like a glass washing machine on
spin like a circus aeroplane ready for take-off it flies like
perpetual motion except it isn't like the endless supply of
light that keeps darkness at bay like a promise of better
things to come before the music runs out of breath.

Crìsdean MacIlleBhàin

MO SHEARMON

Mo shearmon siùbhlach struthlach deifreach,
'na ruith gu cabhagach mar an t-uisge
an dèidh da dhoineann bualadh air bearradh àrd
fad uairean, 's e sireadh gach beàirn is sgoir,
dèin' air a bhith tèarnadh, a bhith
sgaoilte ann am mìltean dhe chuisleannan
beaga, drillseanach, nach cuir cnap-starra
bacadh fada orra – far an tig stac gu oir,
bidh an t-uisge gu h-obann a' stealladh
mar gum b' e falt fuamhair a bh' ann,
ach leis a' cheart ghluasad mhì-fhoighidneach
a bhios aig boireannach 's i tilgeil
a pailteas chiabhan ri taobh
a thuiteam 'nan eas dhe bhoinnean
do-àireamh, làidir, leanmhainneach –
theireadh tu nach fhliuiche idir a bh' ann
ach sreangan, ròpannan anabarrach tana,
cho tana 's gum bi sèideadh beag gaoith
a' fòghnadh gus an toirt às a chèile –
no dh'fhaodadh iad a bhith
'nan cùirtear a tha ceiltinn
chan eil dòigh air nochdadh
ciod e 'n seòrsa thaisbeanadh,
am mireagach no gruamach no co-measgt' –
mo shearmon a shiùbhlas cho grad
nach bi gu lèor a dh'ùin' agad
airson freagairt a chruthachadh nad inntinn,
feumaidh greas a bhith ort
ma tha thu ag iarraidh a ghlacadh!
Mo shearmon a tha mar bhòcan beag crùbte

a gheibh a-steach do chùbaid
nach bu chòir neach eile seach am ministear
a bhith 'na sheasamh innte,
le aodach sìobhalta, oifigeil a' mhinisteir air,
tha e sealltainn dìreach coltach ris
ged a smaoinicheas an coithional
gu bheil e mar gum b' ann air seargadh –
b' àbhaist don mhinistear a bhith coimhead
beagan na b' àirde – agus fhuair
am bòcan gruag bhreugach a dhinn e
sìos air a cheann, bhon a tha fhios ann
falt nam bòcan a bhith cleiteagach, pràbhach
mar nach biodh riamh falt a' mhinisteir
's e nochdadh anns an eaglais air Di-dòmhnaich
agus, san tiota a thòisicheas am bòcan a' bruidhinn,
cha bhi ach treamsgal gun chèill
a' sileadh a-mach bho bhilean sgabach
do bhrìgh 's nach eil na bòcain
eòlach air aon chànan daonnda
ach draoidheachd shònraichte a bhith orra –
is ciamar a dh'fhaodadh draoidheachd phàganach
a bhi èifeachdach san eaglais air Dì-dòmhnaich? –
san tiota seo, nochdaidh am ministear
am measg a' choithional
gun aon chòmhdach air a chom
rùisgte mar san latha a thàinig e dhan t-saoghal
agus bidh e a' ruith 's a' ruith às an eaglais
suas air a' chnoc a tha faisg oirre
fo mhaoim gum faic an sgìreachd uile
cho crìonach neo-theòma 's a tha a cholann
's a bharrachd air sin cho beag 's a tha a ——
(*aon fhacal air a dhubhadh às an seo*)

ach air cho clis, grad-shiùbhlach 's a bhios am ministear
a' ruith dh'ionnsaigh na coille taobh eil' a' chnuic,
fo ionndrainn do bhrìgh 's gu bheil e cinnteach
nach bi e tachairt ri drathais no briogais
air an crochadh gu dòigheil air geug beithe
no sgithich, mar as àbhaist dhaibh bhith crochte
ann am preas-aodaich farsaing
san dachaigh chomhfhurtail aige –
aig a' cheart àm, bidh am bòcan a' leantainn air gu
socraichte
treamsgal an dèidh treamsgail a' tighinn bho bheul
cha robh fhios aige idir e fhèin a bhith
cho sgileil anns an òraideireachd,
tha 'n coithional a' fàs beagan an-fhoiseil
b' àbhaist droch latha no dhà a bhith aig a' mhinistear
cha bhiodh e an còmhnaidh ag ràdh
rudan reusanta no loidigeach
aig amannan bhiodh e doirbh dha-rìribh
aomadh no brìgh a shoisgeulachd a ghlacadh
no aon seagh a b' fhiachail a tharraing a-mach aiste
ach an-diugh tha e dìreach air a chuthach –
bidh am ministear bochd a' faighneachd dheth fhèin
am bu chòir dha, 's dòcha, dàibheadh dhan lochan
ach tha uisgeachan an lochain uamhasach fionnar
b' fheudar dha snàmh gu tìr is a liubhairt fhèin
mu dheireadh thall – air cho bun-os-cionn,
dian, clisgeach 's a bhios am ministear fo oillt
a' saigheadh air adhart 'na dheann-ruith,
cha ruig e 'm feast' an luathas a th' aig
Mo shearmon a bhios uaireannan mar fhiadh sgeunach
nach fhaicear ach plathadh dheth am measg nan
duilleagan

leis cho meata prìobhaideach 's a tha e
agus an uair sin, gun rabhadh idir, mothaichidh tu dha
a' streup suas air a' bhràighe
is smaoinichidh tu gum faodadh sin a bhith 'na aisling
bhon a tha am fiadh cho mòrail, rìoghail, coileanta 'na
    mhosgladh
gach ball dheth a' co-oibreachadh le chèile
mar gun robh e 'g itealaich an àit' a bhith siubhal,
creididh tu cuideachd gum b' fheàrr math dh'fhaodte
nach robh sin ach 'na aisling bho nach bitheadh
modh no inneal ann an uair sin
beud no aimhleas a bhith beantainn dha,
bhiodh e do-ruighinn do-leònadh do-chiùrradh
mar gach rud a chruthaich mac-meanmna
no a thugadh dhuinn ann am bruadar,
cho iomlan, cuimir, do-chlaoidheadh –
agus their thusa riut fhèin:
"Chan eil mise creidsinn ann an Dia sam bith,
chan e Crìostaidh no Muslamach a th' annam,
cha bhi mi toirt mo thaic do ghin dhe na
    seann-teagasgan
mu bhodach aosta, fòirneartach
no mu na h-àitheantan a sgrìobh e sìos
gu bhith gan leantainn leinn
no mu na peanasan sìorraidh
a tha a' feitheamh oirnn
mur a bi sinn strìochdail gu leòr" –
ach their thu cuideachd gur dòcha sin
am faireachdainn a bhiodh aig Dia fhèin
an uair a chruthaich e creutair ùr de fheòl 's de fhuil
gu bhith ga shuidheachadh am bad àraidh dhen
    t-saoghal

Mo shearmon gun fhios dè cho fada 's a tha e dol a bhith
's dòcha gun tèid mi air adhart
gus am faigh Alba neo-eisimeileachd
aig a' cheann thall agus
"Abraibh rium! Sibhse aig a bheil
dlighe air inntreachdainn sa bhùth bheag is crois
a chur sìos ri taobh na beachd as fheàrr leibh
eadar 's gu bheil sibh gealtach no dàna!!
Ciod e an àireamh bhliadhnaichean as fheudar
traoghadh
mus tig an latha miannaichte sin?"
Mo shearmon a bhios 'na dhearbhadh nach eil
coltas sam bith ann gu bheil
an cànan seo fo smachd a' bhàis
a dh'aindeoin na their a' chuid anns an dùisg
a' Ghàidhlig gràin no gamhlas, a bha co-èigneachadh
ar pàrantan is ar seann-phàrantan
gus a mùchadh 's a dearmad,
a dh'aindeoin linn sàrachail fadalach
nuair nach ceadaichte a h-ùisneachadh san oilthigh no
san sgoil,
sam bruidhneadh na fir-teagaisg
eadhon air cuspair Gàidhealach sa Bheurla,
ar cànan fhìn a dh'fhàs 'na adhbhar-maslaidh,
'na chomharradh air bochdainn' is ainfhios
na feadhna chleachdadh ann an cagair e –
smaoinichidh mi air cruinneachadh sgoilearan
bliadhnaichean air ais sa Phòlainn, ann
am baile ris an can na daoine Szczecin
baile Pruiseanach a bh' ann ron chogadh,
Stettin an t-ainm a bh' air, bha suipeir
fhèiseil, mheadhrach a' dùnadh na còmhdhalach,

òigear ann, 's e Sasannach, bha 'g obair
ann an oilthigh san Eadailt, mar a rinn mi fhìn
is mi 'nam òigear, ach nuair a chaidh mi null
a bhruidhinn ris, an ciad rud a thuirt e,
b' e *Not many people speak that language*
agus chuala mise mo ghuth fhìn ag ràdh
gu soilleir, stèidhichte, a' toirt
a thruime sònraichte ri gach aon lide
I – just – haven't – got – the – time
dh'èirich mi air ball is chaidh mi thairis
gu na boireannaich Phòlainneach nach bitheadh,
bha mi cinnteach, claon-bhreith dhen t-seòrs' ac'
's nach iarradh orm bruidhinn mu dheidhinn cuspair
a bhruidhinn mi mu dheidhinn cho tric san àm a
dh'fhalbh
's gu robh e faisg air sgreamh a dhùsgadh annam –
nuair a sheall mi air ais, cairteal uarach às a dhèidh,
bha an t-òigear a' coimhead orm fhathast
iongnadh air aodann, theireadh tu
gun d' fhuair e dìreach sgealp air a ghruaidh
agus smaoinich mise nach robh teagamh ann
nach e dreuchd a tha a' beantainn ruinne fhìn
barrachd foghlaim a sholarachadh do luchd na Beurla
Mo shearmon aig nach bi ach fìor-chorra uair
an aon mhaille eagnaidh, mhion-chùiseach a bhios
uaireannan aig mo leannan 'na ghnìomhachadh –
cha bu chaomh leam sibh a bhith gam thuigsinn ceàrr,
faodaidh a' chùis gu lèir a bhith air a coilionadh
ann an ùine ghoirid cuideachd, mar an turas sin
a bha sinn còmhla nar suidhe aig cuirm-bainnse
is bana-charaid ghràdhaichte air pòsadh aig a' cheann
thall –

theab sinn gach dòchas a chall oir bha
uimhir a chompanaich air a bhith aice, cuid dhiubh
geanalta gu leòr ach cuid eile nach gabhadh
creidsinn gu robh i comasach air feart thaitneach
no tharraingeach sam bith fhaicinn
ann an uilebheist dhen seòrs' ud – chan ann
mu dheidhinn gastachd no ciatachd a tha mi
bruidhinn
ach mu eileamaidean nas bunailtiche riatanaiche
mar, dè cho tric 's a bhios cuideigin ga nighe san
t-seachdain
air neo, gu leòr a mhion-airgead a bhith 'na phòcaid
gus dà chofaidh a phàigheadh, gun iomradh air
notaichean –
bha feasgar àraidh ann a thàinig esan dhachaigh
cha d' fhuair sinn bloigh de chadal gu trì uairean san
oidhche
's e bruidhinn is a' bruidhinn mun chùram a bh' aige
air sgàth na bana-charaid ud – ach a nis bha coltas ann
a h-uile rud a bhith air a seatlaigeadh gu dòigheil,
mo leannan riaraichte mar a bha mise,
sinn nar dithis beagan nar misg, ris an fhìrinn innse
ged nach robh na mìlseanan fhathast air am bòrd a
ruighinn
ach bha am fìon a dhòirt iad nar gloinneachan
blasta gu h-ìre nach fhurast' a chur an cèill –
thuig mi bho mar a bha e sealltainn orm
cha duirt mi facal is mhair esan cuideachd 'na thost,
lean mi e gus an taigh bheag aig na fireannich –
b' e taigh-òsta anabarrach rumail is spaideil a bh' ann,
suidhichte am meadhan pairce mhòir, agus na
caibeineidean

san taigh bheag aibheiseach mar gach uidheam eile,
thachair a h-uile rud gu luath snog, bha sinn fortanach,
cha d' rinn neach eile ar ruighinn fhad 's a bha sinn
    ann –
an dèidh dhuinn an t-èideadh foirmeil aig a chèile
a chur gu mionaideach air gleus, mar a bha feumail,
chaidh sinn air ais gus an talla mhòr
far an robh a' chuideachd uile 'na suidhe –
ach 's ann mu dheidhinn maille shònraichte a thig air
am mòmaidean ainneamh a bha mi 'g iarraidh
    bruidhinn,
neo-ar-thaing gu bheil sinn air uimhir a
    bhliadhnaichean
a chur seachad le chèile, mar as trice is esan
a stèidhicheas ruithim an t-sùgraidh,
chan eil mi cinnteach carson a tha sin a' tachairt,
's a' mhaille ud a' misneachadh faireachdainn annam
cho anabarrach tlachdmhor 's gu bheil e an impis a
    bhith pianail –
faodaidh an ceart ruithim a bhith uaireannan aig
Mo shearmon mar chuthachd aighearach nan
    gobhlan-gaoithe
ann am baile beag san Eadailt air barr cnuic
le bòtharan corrach, caola 's na taighean cho faisg
air a chèile, bidh tu ri plosgartaich mun ruigear leat
mu dheireadh an sguèar a dh'fhosglas air a' mhullach –
mothaichidh tu gu h-obann dha na gobhlanan-gaoithe
gan cur air bhoil le camhanaich an latha
dìreach mar a bhios a' chlann a' ruith
a' glaodhach 's a' brùchdadh a-mach
sna deich mionaidean mus tèid iad dhan leabaidh
an nàdar fhèin a' fàsgadh bhuap'

gach aon luirg air smioralas no guaineas,
a' cuimhneachadh mar a bhrùthas neach spong
gu teann eadar a mheuran gus a h-uile
boinn' a fhliuich' a dh'fhanas innte fhuadachadh –
na gobhlanan-gaoith' gu trang a' figheadh sa
        chamhanaich
lìn aibhisich len goban, a' glacadh
snàthainnean an dorchadais an siud 's an seo,
chan e na cuileagan no na meanbh-bhiastagan
itealach eile a cheapas iad, ach cinn
sreanganan na duibhr' ag udal san adhar,
iad gu dìcheallach a' saigheadh
eadar nam bunnacha-bac, a' teannachadh
na lìn ud anns an tèid an' oidhch' a ribeadh
gu mall rùnaichte dh'aona-ghnothach,
plangaid dhubh a' teàrnadh oirnn uile
a cho-èignicheas eadhon an fheadhainn as
        buaireasaiche
's an-fhoiseile dhen chloinn a ghèilleadh
ris a' chadal a dheòin no a dh'aindeoin
ged nach do dh'fhàs iad fhathast sgith dhe
Mo shearmon . . .

Christopher Whyte

THE WAY I TALK

The way I talk moves, streams and urges,
 rushing along like water when a storm
 has beaten for hours on a high ridge,
 seeking out every gap and notch,
 aching to descend, to be scattered
 in thousands of small, gleaming
 rivulets no obstacle can hold back
 for long – where a crag reaches an edge
 suddenly the water spurts
 like the hair of a giant,
 but with the same impatient gesture
 a woman has tossing her mass of hair
 to one side, so it descends
 in a waterfall of countless
 drops, powerful and insistent –
 you would think it wasn't wetness at all
 but cords, unbelievably thin ropes,
 so thin a gust of wind suffices
 to dishevel them – or else
 they could be a curtain hiding
 who can tell what kind of a performance,
 comical or tragical or both –
 proceeding so fast
 you won't even get time
 to form a question in your mind,
 you'll have to put your skates on
 if you want to catch up with
The way I talk like a little hunched goblin
 who somehow managed to get into the pulpit
 where no one else but the minister

has any right to go,
wearing the minister's fine, official garb
and looking very like him
even if the congregation have the feeling
he sort of shrank –
the minister generally looked
that little bit taller – the goblin also
got hold of a wig he pushed
down onto his head, because everyone knows
goblins have shaggy, unkempt hair
such as the minister's would never be
when he appears in church on a Sunday
and, as soon as the goblin starts talking,
nothing but senseless drivel
comes from his scabby lips
given that goblins are incapable of speaking
any human language whatsoever
unless under a particular spell –
and how could a heathen spell
work in church on a Sunday? –
at that very moment, the minister
appears in the midst of the congregation
naked as on the day he came into the world,
he runs and runs out of the church
up onto the hill close by
terrified that the whole shire will see
how withered and uncoordinated his body is
and besides that, the smallness of his ——
(one word has been crossed out)
but however nimbly and speedily the minister
sprints towards the wood on the far side of the hill,
filled with melancholy because he knows only too well

he won't come upon a pair of trousers or underpants
hanging tidily on the branch of a birch tree
or an ash, the way they usually hang
in the spacious cupboard
of his comfortable home –
meanwhile the goblin chunters on determinedly,
more and more rubbish coming out of his mouth,
he had no idea he was such a splendid orator,
the congregation is getting a bit restless,
from time to time the minister would have a bad day
the things he used to say weren't always
reasonable or logical, at times
it was extremely difficult
to grasp what he might be getting at
or extract any worthwhile meaning from his preaching
but today he has really lost the place –
the poor minister is wondering
if maybe he ought to dive into the loch
though the water is tremendously cold,
he would have to swim to the shore in the end
and hand himself over – however helterskelter,
headlong the panicking minister is
as he shoots onwards like an arrow in his flight,
he'll never match the speed of
The way I talk, at times like a shy deer
you only catch a glimpse of through the foliage
because it is so withdrawn and private
and then, without warning, you see it
climbing up the braeside
and you tell yourself it could be a vision
because its movements are so majestic, kingly,
consummate

all of its limbs working together
as if it were flying rather than running,
and you wonder if it might be better
for it to be a vision, because then
there would be no way or possibility
for harm or malice to reach it,
the deer would be inaccessible, invulnerable
like whatever the imagination produces
or something we see in a dream,
perfect, shapely, invincible –
and you say to yourself:
"I don't believe in any kind of a god,
I am neither a Christian nor a Muslim,
I don't support any of the old doctrines
about a venerable, violent old man
or the commandments he wrote down
for us to follow,
or the eternal punishment
waiting on us
if we are insufficiently obedient" –
but you also say that maybe this
was how God himself felt
after making a creature of flesh and blood
to set down somewhere in the world –
The way I talk, without anybody knowing
how long it is going to continue
maybe until Scotland finally
achieves independence, and:
"Tell me! You who have the right
to enter the little cubicle and put
a cross next to the policies you favour
however courageous or craven you may be!!

How many years still need to pass
before that longed for day arrives?"
The way I talk which proves beyond question
death is not going to triumph over this language
whatever people who regard Gaelic
with distaste or detestation may say,
the ones who forced our parents and grandparents
to suppress it and neglect it,
all through endless, oppressive years
when it couldn't be used at school or at university,
when teachers would use English
even for discussing Gaelic topics
and our language was a source of shame,
a symbol of poverty and ignorance
for the people who spoke it in a whisper –
it makes me think of a conference
I attended years back in Poland,
in a town they call Szczcecin,
a Prussian town before the war,
Stettin was its name then,
the whole business concluded
with a joyous, festive dinner,
there was a young Englishman who taught
at a university in Italy, as I had
when I was young, and when I went over
to speak to him, the first thing he said was
"Not many people speak that language"
and I heard my own voice saying
firmly, steadily, giving due weight
to each single syllable:
"I – just – haven't – got – the – time"
I got up at once and went over

to the Polish women who I was sure
wouldn't have prejudices of this sort
and wouldn't ask me to talk about something
I'd been asked so often in the past
it simply made me feel sick –
when I looked round, a quarter of an hour later,
the young man was still gazing at me
with a surprised expression, you would think
someone had just struck him on the cheek
and I decided there was no question about it,
it's not a job we have to take on,
educating people who promote English –
The way I talk, which very, very rarely
has the same detailed, punctilious slowness
my partner occasionally has when making love –
I wouldn't want you to get me wrong,
sometimes the whole business is over
in a very short time, like the day
we were both sitting at a wedding lunch –
a dear woman friend had finally married –
we practically lost hope, because
she had been with so many guys, some of them
perfectly acceptable, but others
there was no way you could grasp how she could
possibly
find anything pleasing or attractive
in a monster of that sort – I'm not
talking about manners or looks
but about basic, indispensable things
like, how many times in the week somebody washes,
or having enough change in their pocket
to pay for two coffees, not to mention notes –

one night my partner came home,
we didn't get a wink of sleep till three in the morning,
he kept on and on with how worried he was
about our woman friend – and now it looked
as if everything had got settled properly,
my partner was as pleased as I was,
the two of us slightly tipsy to tell the truth,
even though they still had to serve the puddings
but the wine they poured into our glasses
was excellent in a way I can't describe –
I realised from how he was looking at me,
and followed him without saying a word
to the gents', he too was silent –
it was an unusually spacious and posh hotel,
in the middle of a big estate, the toilet
cubicles were as huge as everything else,
we got through it neatly and quickly, we were lucky,
nobody else entered all the time we were there –
once we had adjusted our formal clothes
with due care, we went back
to the big hall where everyone was seated –
but what I wanted to talk about was
the particular slowness that comes over him
in certain rare moments, even if the two of us
have been together for such a long time,
generally he sets the rhythm of our lovemaking,
I couldn't actually say why this happens –
that slowness awakens a sensation in me
so acutely pleasurable it almost hurts –
sometimes there is that same rhythm in
The way I talk, like the exultant craziness
of swallows in an Italian hilltop village

with twisting, narrow lanes and the houses
so close to each other, you are spluttering
before you finally reach the square
that opens at the summit – all of a sudden
you notice the swallows going crazy in the twilight,
just the way children will run around
shouting and exulting in the ten
minutes before they get into bed,
nature itself squeezing out of them
every last trace of energy or mischief,
making you think of how you squeeze a sponge
tightly between your fingers to expel
every last remaining drop of moisture –
the swallows busy weaving in the dusk
a huge net with their beaks, catching
the strands of darkness here and there,
it's not midgies or other flying
insects they intercept, but the ends
of threads of darkness floating in the air
as diligently they dart back and forth
between the eaves, intently weaving
that net tighter, gradually and deliberately
so the night can get trapped in it,
a dark blanket descending on us
that forces even the most tempestuous
and restless of children to yield in the end
to sleep, even if they're still not tired of
The way I talk . . .

translated by Shuggie McCall

Laura Muetzelfeldt

ANNA ON THE WING

Anna looks at her reflection in the darkness and wishes she could sleep. The flashing red of the wing-light pulses against the gloomy layer of cloud, making it closer, suffocating. It's a relief when the plane breaks through into the darkness above. Just beside her, the new moon cuts a sliver into the sky, faint and incomplete. It hangs as if it landed after being tossed into the night. Like a randomly placed fridge magnet, Anna thinks, wanting to straighten it, to line it up with something.

Earlier, her heart pounded as she climbed the stairs to the plane, her feet echoing off the hollow metal frame. It was like she'd just finished one of her races, and she remembered the feel of the foil blanket wrapped around her, tight. When she reached the top step she started to panic, but then a familiar feeling rose up inside her: like guilt. The familiarity of it held her jittery wings safe in its protective hands. Her heart slowed and she felt relieved, on safe ground. She found her seat and, as she sat down, she felt her tummy, soft because she never raced anymore.

Anna looks across at the man sitting beside her. He's holding a coin embossed with a picture of St Christopher and he keeps turning it over and over in his hand. 'To keep me safe,' he explains, then looks over his shoulder for the drinks trolley. The plane hums its slow lullaby and she starts to feel drowsy until, somewhere behind her, a child starts to cry. The sound makes her ribs squeeze and, for a moment, she holds her breath.

This man she is flying to meet, he's the one that thinks she deserves to be happy again. She just feels scared, like she's already done enough living. Anna closes her eyes and imagines the earthy smell of the allotment that she and her husband rented when they were still together. He had looked after the vegetables, and she grew flowers in neat, ordered rows. In her mind, the petals are continuously engaged in their slow, patient eruption, unaware of the miracle she sees in their growth. She counts and recounts the petals on each flower, like the perfect tiny joy of each astonishing fingernail on a pair of wriggling new hands.

The plane flies through frequent turbulence and the fasten seatbelt sign beeps with alarming regularity. An unexpected descent surprises everyone and Anna's seat pushes up, abruptly. She takes a drink from a flimsy plastic glass and gulps down a brand of gin she's never heard of before, but that seems to be working. She looks down at the book of Chekhov's short stories lying open on her lap. She's in the middle of 'The Lady with the Dog', but keeps getting distracted. The last two lines are darker than all the others on the page due to a quirk of printing, and the words shout at her, insistent: 'They both realised that the end was still far, far away and that the hardest, most difficult part was only just beginning.' She folds over the top corner of the page, leans back, and closes her eyes.

Another sudden dip. The man in the seat next to her grips the armrest and Anna places a protective hand on top of her gin. The man beside her turns and tells her he's not scared of flying, he just hates turbulence. He starts asking her questions: Is she married? Any kids?

On planes, Anna often finds herself half-unwillingly, half-willingly, telling the person next to her secrets, just in case the plane crashes. The next time the trolley comes round the man beside her buys her another gin, and she starts talking about why she's on the flight, partly fictionalising her own life. She changes the details, but skims off the truth, and describes as best as she can the raw emotion and nerves that flip her stomach every time she thinks about where she's going, what she's doing. She tells him she's flying to meet someone she's never met before. He's Spanish and he exports oranges. The more she talks, the less real he becomes.

When she wrote and told him she was coming to visit, his reply began: 'Reality takes another step.' She is nervous now, worried that he has fallen for an imaginary version of her – the Anna he met through the website – and that the real Anna will be a disappointment. As a kind of protection, she tries to imagine how the relationship will end, even though it's not even really begun.

It's a tense landing. The man beside her screws up his face and asks Anna if he can hold her hand. Waiting for her suitcase to appear, she wonders if she will recognise the guy she's flying to meet from his photograph, or if he will recognise her. Her navy case is one of the last to arrive, then, feeling sick, she steps out through the terminal doors, into an unfamiliar heat.

*

Two days later, she climbs the stairs to the plane and absent-mindedly finds her seat. It's a window seat, by the wing, again. Anna spends most of the return flight trying not to think about home, wishing they didn't have to land. She fixes her mind on the man who met her at the airport: the first thing he said was, 'You should not have come,' and she shrunk into herself, wounded, stung. He quickly shook his head, saying: 'No, no, no, I mean, you should not travel so far to visit a man you don't really know.' Anna bites her lip; it was the first of several confusions to do with language, and she worries what else he might have misunderstood.

Waiting for the drinks trolley, she gets out her digital camera and jumps from photo to photo, like stepping stones through the time they spent together. She starts to catalogue her memories from the trip. Although everything happened only in the last two days, it is almost an act of archaeology, or archiving; it is already in the past.

When she gets to the photo of the cathedral, she remembers the brash sound of her footsteps on the cold, marble floor. She paused in front of a shrine and he explained, 'for people who are under sin.' She lent forward, and read the price it cost to light up one of the electric candles. 'Under sin – that sounds so terminal, like a curse.'

The next photo shows the bright circus yellow of the pigeon they came across in the city square. He told her it was a retired racing pigeon, stained yellow when it was owned, and now unaware how it stood out. 'After a while, they give them their freedom,' he said. She nodded, unconvinced.

Anna skips forward until she gets to a photo of a line of floats stretching out into the sea. On the second afternoon, they drove to a wildlife reserve and walked along the jetty with the reserve on one side, the sea on the other. After about ten minutes, they stopped to look at a black and white puddle of fluttering birds. They watched as a chain reaction of aggressive flapping moved from bird to bird as if they were playing catch with an itch.

'Why are they shaking like that?' she asked.

'It either means war, or it is the male trying to mate, I guess.'

Further along, flamingos kicked their coat-hanger legs as they fished, capsized with heads underwater. They walked in silence and the sound of Anna's shoes rang out, jarring with the landscape around them.

They kept walking until they got to the end of the jetty where two concrete blocks marked the end of the reserve and the start of the rough water of the sea. He sat on one of the blocks and she wandered over to look at the old, derelict harbour. She photographed broken things: boats half-submerged with stones at the bottom; enamel flaking off signs stuck in the water; painted-over graffiti. When he wasn't looking, she took a photograph of him with a broken windmill as the backdrop, then walked over to where he was sitting. She stood facing him, buried her hands in the pockets of his hooded top, and there was a thrill when his fingers found the skin at the base of her spine.

On the walk back, Anna pointed her camera up at the sky and tried to snap birds in flight. She flicks through photos of ducks, flamingos, and strange-looking seagulls that travelled in pairs. She noticed that flamingos always looked more pink in the distance, and wondered why.

The next shot is from the hotel balcony and she remembers lying on the twin beds, side-by-side. Things were awkward when they got back to the hotel at first, but then they were suddenly cosy and very sleepy and fell asleep almost touching. Anna woke up half-falling down the gap between the two single beds in the darkness, and moved over to his side. His hand gradually smoothed away the diminutive swell of her belly, just one of the places her body changed. Somebody's stomach rumbled and she wasn't sure whether it was hers or his.

Later, the sound of a baby crying travelled along the hotel corridor and she didn't realise that tears were falling down her cheeks until he asked her what was wrong. Then she told him everything, without pausing for breath, like they were strapped in side-by-side on a plane that was hurtling towards the ground.

She tried to explain. It was her second marathon: she remembers crossing the finish line and thinking the stickiness between her thighs was sweat. Her heart was still pounding when an official tapped her on the shoulder, not realising what the blood meant. Then there was shouting and panic as she was rushed to the medical tent.

Her grief has an exact size, she cradles it, and carries it everywhere she goes. Losing it would be unbearable, another loss. Before Richard left he threatened tenderly: 'Enough is enough.' As he cried, he endlessly called her name as if he was trying to wake the person he loved from a bad dream. Getting the allotment was his idea; he thought it would be good for them to have something to do.

One day Richard lost his temper with the silence and said out loud, but not really at her, 'You ran. I told you not to run.' With that, he turned and walked out of her life without saying another word. Secretly she had been glad to be rid of him; he was taking up too much of her time with all of his questions and worried glances. He didn't understand: there were things she had to think about, and she had to think about them constantly otherwise she was worried she'd forget.

The seatbelt sign is switched on and the pilot announces that they will shortly be arriving at their destination: local time is 15:35 and the weather is overcast. As the plane flies nearer home, Anna struggles to hold onto the feeling of freedom he gave her and the certainty of what just happened begins to fade. She thinks of the flamingos she saw, pinkish in the water, but flying grey against the sky. 'Will I see him again?' she thinks and, puzzled, repeats the word 'him'. Then she thinks back over the weekend and realises she never once said his name, not even in her head.

The plane wobbles. Anna looks down at her digital camera and realises, horrified, that she has been deleting every photo after she has looked at it. She's annoyed at first but, after a while, she feels something like relief. Saying goodbye at the airport already seems a lifetime ago. As the plane lands, she struggles to try and remember what he looked like, but can't.

Colette O'Connor

LOOKING AT AN EIGHTEENTH-CENTURY ATLAS

This paper worn soft as skin
unspools nations to the edges
of conquest. I find the map of
Scotland, point to the space where
here isn't written. She says
it was a mistake to come here
and by *here* she means *now*.
She has retreated to the margins
of the once known. She dreams
of taking the A1 south to 1943,
where she would step from the car
unassisted, hop cracks in the bomb
pocked pavement, whistling
that song that floats up through
memory again and again like
the moon's reflection shivering
from the depths of a plum dark lake.

Niall O'Gallagher

BLÀTH NA BEALTAINE

Sìn do làmh
gun glac thu blàth
na craoibhe àird'
    bàn-dearg, mìn

a thig am fàs
an earraich thràith
nach mair ach là
    mus searg i

(gach seilean làn
neactair is àis
mar bheachaibh àl
    na bàn-righinn)

is tu, a ghràidh,
le lasgan tlàth
is faite-gàir'
    nad gheal-rìbhinn.

Dèan dàil
gum breacadh sgàil
do bhathais bhàn
    clàr do leth-chinn

is i ri danns
a-measg nan crann
air d' chraicinn anns
    a' ghàrradh bhinn

gach duilleag gràis
cho maiseach dàn
air dath bu ghnàth
　　do phlaide fight'

de chanach àis
na leabaidh bhlàith
gum faigh thu tàmh
　　is cadal innt'.

Sin do làmh
cailleag as àill'
is tu aig bàrr
　　mo ghàirdean fhìn

le teachd na ràith
a dh'fhalbh tràth
ge b' i a dh'fhàg
　　blas meala dhith

fantainn san àil'
mar ghealladh fàis
san t-sneachda bhàn
　　is beatha ùr-bhrist'

is gabh am blàth
a b' àill leat, ghràidh,
a nighean, fhlaith
　　na crann-sirist'.

Latha na Bealtaine, 2018

BEÀRNAIN-BHRÌDE

Thoiream flùr airson do chinn
bheir mi dhutsa beàrnan-Brìd';

don chrùn agad mo ghuidhe
airson flùir bhig òr-bhuidhe.

As t-earrach tha iad cho pailt
ri flùr sam bith fon iarmailt,

far am bi aonan a' fàs
fàsaidh iad sa h-uile h-àit'.

'S ann mar sin a tha mo ghràdh
mar na flùraichean òrdha:

cumanta, ach chan ann lag
do na bheir, no gheibh, buidheag;

's ann le gràdh na h-ighne big'
a tha an dìthean coisrigt',

an tairgseadh a bheir a' bhrìgh
do na bha roimhe dìblidh,

mar am flùr, no mar an dàn,
's e cho gnàthach ri beàrnan

-Brìde dh'fhàsas mòr is àrd
am mac-meanmna an t-saobh-bhàird.

Mar sin, thar gach lus' sa lios,
bheir mi dha mo ghràdh dìleas,

don bheàrnan-Brìde is dhi
as àille na cainnt filidh,

a chionn 's nach eil gràdh cho mìn
na th' aig athair dha nighinn

gur buidhe dhòmhsa fon ghrèin
mar òr-ghruagan m' eudail fhèin.

Pip Osmond-Williams

TANTALLON ROAD

When you try to leave me
in the morning
apologetically
I trace the ring of Apollo
around my finger
the Mount of Venus
where you kissed me coarse
and sweet in the dark
and then my arm
the crescent of my ear and eyelid
the flush of my hips and then
back to my palm.
If I stretch for you
in your good blue suit
it's only because I want to tell you
that I know you've heard me pray
sweet Jesus
for temperate days
but in the dawning of
your muted room
I would rather you
melt me on your tongue
like a sugar cube
sweat like manuka honey
dripping from the spoon.
Come bury yourself like cutlery
in the crook of me.
It's still early
you could just close the door
and leave the coffee.

Alycia Pirmohamed

EBB & FLOW

How much thirst
must have interlaced
with oil and wax
to build maroon lips –

I am uncovering
the stranger
in my body
            like this:

lift   swab   inoculate—

A scientific detangling:
my heart (73% water)
my lungs (83% water)

my memory
of maroon mouths,
molecules of water
(unquantifiable)
            simmering –

If I am at least
50% water,
I must be
            almost a river:

lift   swell   seethe—

How being a percentage
of anything
means being without

cattail (typha latifolia),
or heron (ardea cinerea),
or the current

or something not yet
known.

Does everything
parted by water long
for an antonym?

If I am 50% river
am I opposite
of a river too –

almost river/
almost earth/
almost sky.

Martin Raymond

ONE WEEK IN THE WHITE CITY

When I first spotted Darko in the business lounge of Frankfurt Airport I didn't know he was going to ambush me with the past. He was unmistakable – the body of a grandee, the face of an eager child. His glasses flashed in the lights. Everything was shiny here, the edges of the furniture, the bottles, the covers of the magazines. He was laughing with two colleagues. Or rather he was laughing on his own. In their low armchairs the other two were serious men, angular in expensive suits. Leather laptop bags lay around them like territorial markers.

I waited to see when he'd acknowledge me. I was enjoying my gin and tonic. Next to the tiny table my cabin-friendly bag was poised to go on its toy wheels. As I stirred my miniature lemon peel he waved across. I could see the two men narrow their eyes, curious. He was out his seat quickly before I had a chance to go over to their encampment.

'Gor. Don! How are you?' He split my name emphatically in two, justified revenge for the way I'd mangled all the names in Belgrade. His grip was painful.

'What are you up to here?'

'My associates and I,' he indicated that I had his permission to sit down again in my own seat while he remained standing, 'are on our way to Chicago. We have a possible investor there.' He waited for me to be impressed. I nodded, a man of the world.

'Sounds good,' I said.

'Yes, yes.' There was urgency to tell me now. 'You know my project? A social development to harness the energy of our young people. They learn on the job as they work in the community. They earn less but learn more.'

His associates didn't look like philanthropists or community activists, but you can never tell.

'We are going to see a possible investor, one of our diaspora who left after the war. Where are you going?'

I told him I was going to run a workshop in Manchester, having been at a conference in Magdeburg. He was unimpressed.

'I've never been there. Have you been back in Belgrade?'

I shook my head. 'That's five years?'

'Maybe more,' said Darko, glancing over at his compatriots. 'Listen Gor-don I must get back, you know how it is?'

Indeed I did. We shook hands again. More pain.

As he turned I said, 'Do you ever see Maja or Andjela?'

He stopped and for the first time gave me eye contact.

'Not since I left the health department, but I hear that Maja is now practicing medicine in Oregon. Andjela has retired.'

'Her house by the sea?'

He looked at me from behind his round glasses.

'Maybe.'

'Well if you do see either of them . . .'

He cut me off.

'Sure, sure. Hey – ciao.'

He was gone, and I was back with my drink, thinking about the strange week in Belgrade. Beo Grad, the white city, with the signs in Roman and Cyrillic script it felt like a town on the border. It didn't take me long to work out that the frontier was part of the culture, with the barbarians always just beyond the trees. What did I know about the war? That the Serbs were the aggressors? Atrocities happened. That was about it. A visiting trainer has to pick up the culture quite quickly, understand what can and can't be said. Which is where Maja and Andjela came in.

'Gor-don, not this slide, I think,' Maja would say as I ran through my proposed routine.

'Not the exercise?

'No. They have asked you because of your knowledge, they don't want to sit about talking, they can do that at their work. They want you to tell them.'

'No group games?'

'No. No games. You are the expert. They will listen. And make notes.' Her eyebrows were elegant and serious. Her hair like autumn trees reflected on water.

Andjela, her boss, would sit at the back of the sessions. Beyond the ranks of doctors, nurses and administrators, I'd see her iron grey hair, nodding, or not, as I overlooked the irony of explaining smoking prevention strategies to professionals who had witnessed a decade of war.

After the sessions Andjela would provide me with detailed feedback. Maja would take a deferential step back when she spoke.

'Don't mention the war' is a tired joke, but here it seemed like sound advice. In every session, at every moment, there was a gentle undertow, an unspoken acknowledgement of what had gone on here. I was part of the re-building, the re-establishment of civil infrastructure, the only way to prevent a slide back into the bad ways.

'Local radio is a good channel for health-related messages. You have a network of local radio?' I'd opine beside my screen.

'No. No local radio,' a formidable physician replied from the gloomy edge of the meeting room. 'But we have still from the old days a network of local TV stations, fourteen around the country.'

'These were for propaganda, under the regime,' Andjela said later, 'you understand?'

I nodded. Without understanding one bit.

Darko was always there at the beginning and the end of sessions. He was too busy, even then, he explained, to attend all day. He was a man from the ministry, there to report back on just how well things were going. If there were any issues, any problems at all, then I was to tell him.

'Maja has got it all under control,' I'd say. 'Perfect organisation. And then Andjela is usually there too.'

'Yes. But Gor-don,' Darko would grab my arm, gently, 'if there is anything that is a difficulty you will let me know. This is important for my department, you know this?'

I nodded. But then I was only familiar with bureaucracies that were merely irritating.

Back in the lounge Darko was currently deep in conversation with the two men. They'd glanced my way initially while he explained who I was, but as I was neither threat or opportunity I didn't deserve much attention. Now Darko was working again, switching eye contact from one to the other, selling, pitching. I was almost sorry for them with nine hours to O'Hare ahead of them. Darko had been wasted in the health department. How useful he was to the government back then wasn't clear. I wasn't asked back. So Darko's reports couldn't have contained many five-star reviews.

Not that my week was grim. After long training days was never left in my hotel room for long. Darko never initiated it but he was always there for evenings out at restaurants and even a trip to the ballet, booked and organised by Maja with Andjela's endorsement. The cuisine was located somewhere between the wide beetroot fields of the steppes and the olive hills of the Mediterranean.

One evening we went to an old-style hotel full of presences from both the Hapsburg and Soviet empires. Across the street was the dark bulk of the Ministry of Defence building. It had been left in its bombed-out, blackened state to make a point to visitors from the West, people like me. Each concrete floor of 1960s brutalism was compacted down on the next. A tangle of rusting reinforcing steel and wiring was squeezed out at every gap – the entrails. I'd never been to a city that had been freshly bombed before. From my restaurant chair the Ministry building was just over Andjela's shoulder, out through the window and across the traffic. She let me gaze for a course or two as we chit-chatted health policy and budgets. Then she intercepted my eye-line.

'That was just one bomb. A cruise missile. Boof.' She smiled. 'Powerful?'

Darko was looking for a waiter. Maja seemed to check something with Andjela, then said,

'We've been bombed by everyone. Our beautiful city.'

'The Turks,' said Andjela.

'The Russians,' said Maja.

'The Bulgars.'

'The Soviets.'

'The Germans.'

'Twice.'

'And you!' Andjela almost laughed.

'NATO,' said Maja. 'Not you, personally.'

'Don't worry,' said Andjela, 'we don't hold you responsible for the humanitarian bombing of us.' She smiled, Maja smiled, eyes wide, teasing me without a trace of humour.

'These were terrible months.' For once Maja cut over her boss. 'my husband you know is an obstetrician. The hospitals . . .'

'And electricity and water plants,' said Andjela.

'. . . were NATO targets. All the expectant mothers were told not to go to the hospital. So he had to go to them. All over the city on nights of the raids.'

Both women leaned in on the table. I wasn't looking out the window now.

'And my worry was the bridge.'

'You know the main bridge over the river?' said Andjela.

I did. I'd crossed it in the taxi from the airport. A slim concrete arc, it soared high above the valley of the Danube. I considered the long drop.

Maja demanded eye contact now, her brows narrowing,

'And that bridge was your target, the main one,' she paused and straightened her knife and fork. They were heavy, well used, with thousands of tiny scratches on the polished surfaces.

'Every night in raids he'd go out with his team, with the oxygen to the mothers, always over the bridge and I'd be at home with my children listening to the bombs.'

I couldn't think of any words, so I made a noise, sympathetic, neutral.

'You know Gordon,' said Andjela, 'you feel these bombs before you hear them, through your bones.' The two women's heads were touching now, willing me to understand something that was beyond me.

'That was the past.' Darko reappeared, suddenly. Rescue. 'Now we are here because of the future.'

But they were waiting for me to respond.

'How long did it go on for?' I said.

'The bombing? Until we negotiated,' said Andjela.

'Until they negotiated,' said Maja. 'But we two,' her eyes moved to Andjela, 'were moved, to run a hospital up in the hills away from the city.' She stopped abruptly.

Then Darko was calling for the bill and we were out on the street and I was off in a taxi to my bleak hotel. All that night the lift arrived on my floor with a thump like concrete falling.

On the last night we were back at the same restaurant. The white tables like snowy fields. We all drank to the success of the training, and my return, even Darko, who presumably knew by then that I wasn't coming back.

'So you both worked in the same hospital, in the hills?' I said over the fish.

'Yes,' said Maja, 'I was Medical Supervisor and Andjela was Director.'

Andjela was looking down at her plate, one hand on the salt cellar, a pre-Soviet object that weighed more than a half-finished bottle of wine. But I pressed on, blindly.

'So was it safer there, away from the NATO bombing?'

'Nowhere is safe in a war,' said Andjela. It was almost a whisper, polite and full of absolute contempt for me. 'We were the cruel people to you, aren't we?' She paused but not so I could reply. 'We did all the wicked things. Serbia. That's what you think,' Her pale eyes caught the light. 'But you didn't live in it. What do you know?' The salt cellar cracked on the table – a single shot.

It was Darko, of course who stepped in.

'You see, we have been through bad times here. I know you understand, appreciate the stress of that. In health-care we're not soldiers but we see things.'

Maja said nothing. Andjela smiled – pure ice. I apologised. We were all professionals, there would be no stumping off. But the warmth we had was over, and I was hurt. Maja nodded gravely as Andjela told us about her second home on the Montenegrin coast and Darko bought a round of plum brandy.

'The taste of Serbian hills, Gor-don, better than whisky.'

And the next morning I was in a taxi and home and on to the next piece of work. I mined the trip ruthlessly, stories to tell, a spurious knowledge of war zones – or ex-war zones. But I never forgot Maja and Andjela and their strange closeness, their heads touching over the table, finishing each other's sentences, their hospitality, and how they suddenly turned on me.

Darko and his collaborators were starting to stir, rounding up their bags, ready to move on. Darko went back to the free drinks for a last refill and I had a sudden need to join him, to reconnect with that week.

'So, Manchester awaits?' We stood side by side at the table with the bottles.

'Then home.'

'Home is always there.' Darko swilled an inch of vodka at the bottom of his tall glass. 'You know you shouldn't judge these two women.'

'I never judge.' I began to wish I'd stayed in my seat. Darko put his dirty glass down among the ranks of identical clean glasses.

'In that hospital in the hills they got cut off. You see, beyond help. All these children they had there with mental issues – what's the word?'

'Learning difficulties.'

'Yes Gor-don, difficulties. They couldn't get out. You know what had happened in other places like that when an army got there? You imagine? The hatred. So together they had to save them from that. There was only one way to save them from the soldiers, from the hate. Maja and Andjela together, alone, all the nurses gone but plenty drugs.'

We stood together in the gleaming space, facing the drinks table, two men in suits waiting for flights.

'So one night they worked through the wards, with the drugs. Then they waited patiently for the soldiers to arrive. But they didn't arrive, Gor-don, they were ordered to the south and passed through the next village.'

'I see.'

'Yes?' He raised an eyebrow above his glasses. 'There were no questions asked, it was war. They did what they thought they had to do. You understand now? You were getting on a plane, that next day, home. They had that night in the hospital with them forever.' He paused. 'My flight.' He nodded towards the board, the plate glass wall and the open sky beyond.

I'd always thought of Darko as a man-child, enthusiastic and ruthless. They'd all seemed so innocent, somehow purged by war. But as I thought of Maja in the white-fenced suburbs of Oregon, Andjela in her dacha, watching the sea, I knew I was the ingenue with nothing to teach and everything to learn. My gate hadn't been called but I wanted to move, out into the wide glossy walkways, towing my little bag.

Calum Rodger

PRESS X TO JUMP IN MASS GRAVE

centre the left-stick
to calibrate your being-in-the-world
when the gold stars encircle the blue dot press B

you are a citizen of Glasgow, Scotland
four months after the Brexit vote
rapidly tap Y to not go back to sleep

rapidly tap A to not smoke a cigarette
hold B to shiver; tap X to curse
suddenly again the mornings are cold

toggle L to open your personal assistant
use the D-pad to listlessly scroll
for updates on in-game developments

(the game adjusts in real-time
according to players' behaviour)
tap A or B or Y or whatever

toggle L; press X to get out of bed
hold Y and tap B to get dressed
rapidly tap A to not smoke a cigarette

press B to hope it's all a bad dream
hold R to imagine a hand
press X to despair, despair
press it as hard as you can

use the left-stick to control your movement
and the right-stick to look around you
press X to interact with objects and people

get to the bus stop before 7:30
hold R to tense up your neck in your collar
press Y to see the leaves fall where they may

select some loose change from your inventory
press A to say 'morning' or B to stay mute
when you find a free newspaper, press X to read

hold Y to look for cheat codes in the headlines
(careful, I've known players get banned for less)
to grit your teeth tap A and B together

note the two health bars in the corner of your view
the first is the game world and the second is you
both are outwith player control

hold A to recall the lyrics
of your favourite band as a teen
'life's like a video game with no chance to win'

press B to hope it's all a bad dream
hold R to imagine a hand
press X to despair, despair
press it as hard as you can

the start button opens your map
so that you can locate yourself in the world
here is fog of war; here are borders

press start to return to your immediate environment
use the right-stick to look around you
as if searching for a glitch an avatar could slip through

or press all the buttons together
as if to escape from the game
look: nothing happens; but try it again

re-centre the right-stick
don't press anything now
count the minutes of the in-game world

Brexit means Brexit
press X means press X press B means press B
press Y means press Y means press Y means press Y

tap B to drop the controller
hold R to refuse to play
press X to perform no function
press it to stay, to stay

you have arrived at your destination
rapidly tap A to not smoke a cigarette
press X to interact with objects and people

Cynthia Rogerson

SOUTH VAN NESS

I had a room in an old woman's basement that Fall. I had to enter through the garage, and the room was dark and pine-panelled. There was a tiny bathroom but no kitchen. That was fine. I'd burned down the kitchen in the last place I'd rented a room. Clearly, I was not to be trusted in kitchens. There'd been Sufi dancers in that other place, and they'd refused to be angry with me even though the fire had destroyed all their vegan cooking equipment. I couldn't handle that. I needed punishment.

I'd just turned eighteen. A few months ago, when I was still living at home, I'd slept with the new neighbour down the street whom my father had specifically told me to avoid. I'd knocked on his door and asked if he had any rolling papers. Within fifteen minutes, we were both naked and he was walking around the house with me pinioned on him, my legs around his back, arms around his neck. It was like an erotic piggyback game. I was not petite, he must have been athletic. My face was raw and pink later because his beard had exfoliated it. I went back home, transparently fornicated, and my father's face got very red. Then he threw his wine at my face and said:

'Get out!'

I marched straight out of the house and hitchhiked to a friend's house. The wine was white, and as soon as it dried there was no sign he'd even thrown it. Within a day, I'd found the Sufi house and moved out of my old bedroom. In front of my tearful five-year-old sister and my envious sixteen-year-old brother, I walked out of my childhood home clutching a duffle bag full of clothes and shoes and books I considered good. I do not remember my mother in this. She may have been there. She was self-effacing and undemanding, but loved us continually. She was probably was there in the hall, watching me head off into the unknown. I have no idea what she felt. Perhaps she was asking herself if she was supposed to cling to me, and beg me not to go. She was too shy to do anything so demonstrative, but she might have pictured it just the same. My father had removed himself proudly to the garage during my exit. *My house, my rules.* He had a point. I was a brat.

In my new life ten miles away, I started junior college and worked as a waitress in an old folk's home and hitchhiked everywhere. I got C-minuses at college that first semester. I was a terrible waitress and asked to be demoted to the less stressful job of busboy. Hitchhiking was the only thing I was good at. I'd perfected it the previous summer in Europe, where I thumbed (occasionally on the wrong side of the road) through Ireland, England, Germany, Switzerland and France. It was a revelation that I could go anywhere for free. It was mostly fun, aside from being raped twice by the same man in the back of his van. He'd parked in some menacing forest in France in the middle of the night, and I was more afraid of being abandoned there than dealing with his lust, which was quickly sated. Despite his refusal to accept my *no*, it was likely he did not consider me raped at all. He dropped me off on the outskirts of a small village. I was bow-legged and sticky thigh-ed, and I stunk. I was not ready to stick out my thumb again, so just kept walking and then I smelled baking bread. It was dawn. There were no cars, no people, just the bread aroma wafting out of a bakery window. I stood on the dusty path below the window and inhaled it. I was not hurt. Nothing important had been stolen – I still had my passport and some money. The sun was shining, and I was an American suburban girl in a quaint French village. I closed my eyes to the sun for a second, and when I opened them the baker was holding out a baguette from the open window. He was not young. He had a fat man's face, rosy and round. He did not want my money and said something softly in French, which I already knew was the most beautiful language in the world.

He blew me a kiss, and I said *merci* and walked away. The bread restored everything.

*

Aside from that night in the French forest, plus a few truck drivers taking out their predictable penises, hitching was a safe way to travel. It was fun, too. I made lots of friends. I met a man who called himself Morris the Minnow in Galway and camped with him on Innismore. I formed a trio of hitchers with a Jewish woman from New York and a home counties boy called Julian, and we hitched from Paris, right across the channel on a car ferry and up to his parent's ancestral pile in Hampshire. My address book was crammed with new addresses, where I was assured a place to sleep if I was in the area. I had not made a success of high school, but hitching was a place I did not feel a failure. I loved standing by the road alone, waggling my thumb at drivers. I had found my gift. All that danger was strangely relaxing.

*

But that was months ago, and now I was living my new life ten miles from home. One day, after my busboy shift, I was picked up by a tall fair man in a white van. I was on my way to the city to sit in Café Trieste and feel soulful. It was a very big van, comfortable and clean. The back was full of chunks of foam rubber.

'What's all the foam rubber for?'

'I manufacture furniture,' he explained. When I stared blankly, he continued. 'I have a foam furniture factory.' He smiled with very white teeth.

He had a pretty face, like a woman. His blue eyes seemed honest and trustworthy. No beard. He looked like he might not be able to grow a decent beard, his skin was so soft and white. His hair was strawberry blond and hung to his shoulders, not straight but not curly either. Fluffy. He looked old, but not old like my father.

'Cool,' I said. 'Do you have any rolling papers?' That was my only line.

We ended up at his factory on South Van Ness and 15th Street, which was near the freeway overpass. No houses on this block – just warehouses and flop houses. A fifteen-minute walk from Union Square, it was a side of the city I'd not seen. We entered and immediately there were stairs – steep and dark. I didn't hesitate a second, but I was aware this was a point at which caution would be considered appropriate. I kept taking my own emotional temperature to see if I would feel frightened. At the top, he showed me where he slept – the factory was also his home. The walls of his bedroom were comprised entirely of yellow foam rubber somehow attached to the structure of the building. I couldn't see any nails. The outer layer of the foam rubber, which was about ten inches thick, was smooth and almost hard, as if it had been singed. The door was another wedge of foam rubber that you had to fold back and then slide your body through. Inside was a bed-sized piece of foam rubber on the floor, made up into a bed with the usual bed things – sheets, blankets and pillows. There were some clothes neatly folded in a corner of the room on the floor, which was also foam rubber. It was a padded cell with a single bulb hanging from the ceiling, but oddly cosy. Maybe it was the yellowness and the way it smelled of Johnson's Baby Powder. Outside the room was the kitchen. This was a wooden plank over two saw horses, on which sat a can opener and dozens of cans of tuna and sweetcorn, a few plates, bowls and cups. Cutlery stuck out of an empty sweet corn can. There was also a jumbo-size box of Corn Flakes and some boxes of powdered milk.

'No stove?'

'Raw food is better for you.'

'No sink?'

'There's one in the bathroom,' he said and smiled kindly, as if it was a silly question. Why would any house need more than one sink?

All this time, he was kind of dancing around me on the balls of his feet, his long skinny legs propelling him around in a bouncy way. He seemed delighted I was there, albeit bewildered. Nothing he did set off alarms. I liked his minimalism. He was, it turned out, thirty years old and, according to him, his foam rubber factory was worth a million dollars.

For foreplay, he showed me the factory beyond his bedroom. There was a rough-hewn balcony, which we stood on, and below on the ground floor was a veritable swimming pool of foam rubber. Then he climbed over the railing and leapt down. I followed. Falling on so much foam was like falling into cake. It made me giggle.

The sex was not memorable, but then I was still so immature. It was like smoking a joint but not knowing how to inhale. Later, he dropped me off at an onramp for 101 north, and I was back in my pine-panelled basement room within an hour.

*

I kept failing at college. Perhaps my mother was wrong and I was not a genius. I was always too tired to study, and my salary was not stretching as far as I thought it would. I was working full time, and I didn't see how I could make more money. I liked the idea of a philosophy or an English degree, but I was not prepared to make many sacrifices to get one.

I didn't have a boyfriend. I wasn't sure Foam Man would describe himself as my boyfriend, though we'd met up three more times. There was a boy I met at college who showed me how to give a blowjob one day. We did it in my pine-panelled room. It was hard to keep quiet, but we had to try because the old lady upstairs could throw me out. I hid how disgusted I was, because he didn't seem to think it was disgusting at all. Besides, it seemed a useful life skill to acquire.

'Move your hand like this, just at the base,' he whispered.

'Like this?' I whispered back.

'Yeah. But you're not sucking. You're slurping. Suck.'

'Like this?'

'Ouch! Goddammit.'

I gagged at one point. I was C-minus at blowjobs too. I kept clearing dirty tables, daydreaming in classes, and hitching home on a regular basis to see my family. The tension had evaporated within days of my leaving, and now they were always glad to see me. Even my father. We enjoyed each other's conversation too much to stay alienated. I was waiting for my life to begin, I guess. I was making lots of mistakes, and not having as much fun as most people my age seemed to be having. Life was generally a little flat. I was waiting to know who I would be, but mainly I think I was waiting for someone to love.

*

One night in my narrow bed, I was listening to the radio and a Harry Nilsson song came on. It was a popular song. *No I can't forget this evening, or your face as you were leaving, but I guess that's just the way the story goes. You always smile, but in your eyes your sorrow shows. Yes it shows.* A curious thing happened as I listened. My chest seemed to fill up. What had seemed dead before, was now alive. I pictured myself as both the sad-eyed leaver and the broken-hearted one left behind. It was corny, but also painful because it seemed to be saying something true. Lovers sometimes lacked the power to hang on to loved ones, and worse – sometimes loved ones left, even when they knew they were loved.

*

I can't live, if living is without you. I can't live, I can't give anymore. Had I ever loved anyone that much? Had I ever been loved that much? No, I had not. Did I want to? Yes, it turned out I did. But who to pour this love into, and who to be the beloved of? Why, Foam Man of course! He was not perfect, but he was the only one I could think of. I fixed on his face, his shoulders, his funny way of walking like he was bouncing. I got up, got dressed, and left the house. It was late, maybe ten-thirty p.m. I was exploding with resolution. It felt great to be following an impulse and not analysing anything. Thinking, I decided, was over-rated. I walked to the onramp for 101 south and stuck out my thumb. I wore my usual outfit – hip-hugging bell-bottom jeans, a peasant blouse (no bra), and a corduroy jacket which had belonged to my father.

I quickly got a lift to the city, and then stuck out my thumb again on Lombard. The air was cool, and the foghorn was mourning away. Standing in a bus stop with my thumb out, I felt the vestiges of fear watching groups of men loitering outside a corner bar. One of the men kept hawking and spitting, and another kept laughing like a hyena. Finally, a car pulled over, the driver rolled down his window and said:

'Hey, you working?'

'Working? No,' I said, puzzled, and got in his car.

He turned and stared at me, and I waited for him to say something else.

'Are you going down Van Ness?' I finally asked. 'I need a lift to 15th and South Van Ness.'

'Oh, what the hell,' he suddenly said, and pulled out into traffic.

*

My swollen heart had waned a little but when I heard his footsteps coming down, it began to flutter again. I'd never experienced emotion as a physical object, something like a thick liquid in my chest, something even more delicious than that French baguette last summer. Was this love? I decided it was, and also that I would not require more than this chance to love someone. Being a beloved would be icing on the cake.

'Jesus! What are you doing here? It's past midnight.'

'Yeah, well. I just suddenly wanted to see you.' There was an awkward pause, so I added, 'I was in the neighbourhood.'

I couldn't articulate the romance of my impulse. It all sounded impossibly juvenile in spoken words. But surely he'd recognise the dramatic gesture for what it was? He was so much older, he must know all about dramatic gestures.

'Huh. Well, come on up and get warm. I've got some peppermint tea. Then I've got some paperwork to do.'

Peppermint tea? Where was the wordless embrace? The sense of rightness?

But within a month, I'd moved out of the pine-panelled basement and into the foam rubber factory. I dropped out of college, but still hitched to the old folk's home to busboy till I had enough money to fly back to Europe. If I wasn't going to get a degree or a career or a beloved, I might as well travel. From the beginning, when I moved in with Foam Man, it was understood. He offered no mushy talk, and neither did I. My midnight visit was never referred to. This was my base camp while I saved up to travel. A temporary base. He did not ask for money and I did not offer it. I didn't even pay for my share of our daily tuna fish. We never drank, though sometimes shared a joint at bed-time. He had such a long lanky body, it was nice to feel entirely wrapped in it. We tended to read in bed, more than do anything else.

*

The day came.

'I've got my ticket.'

'Yeah?'

'I leave next weekend.'

'Wonderful. You must be excited.'

This was exactly how he was supposed to behave, but my heart sank. The preferred response, I realised with sickening clarity, was: *Please don't go*. I willed Foam Man to say those words, or any version of that sentiment. My throat became sore with unshed tears, as the time of my departure grew near. It was all tragic and unnecessary. I could feel my life teeter between completely different paths. The known or the unknown. But it wasn't really teetering. It was timidly waiting for choice to be removed. All he had to say was *please stay*, and I would stay. Like the lyrics that had propelled me out of my bed six months earlier and sent me to his door, I now had the eyes with hidden sorrow, and I was leaving. If he would only notice and burst into song. *I can't live, if living is without you.*

But he did not, and I left.

Mark Russell

MEN, AS A MATTER OF FACT

About war, they say, there is nothing new to serve with a first-class mayonnaise. It is as common to prohibit the production, conveyance, and sale of popular novels, as it is to ban the use of cars and public transport to those in low-income families. Which is to say, not very common. But it is common for men to hanker after the legitimisation of these options. Especially the one with the novels. Men would very much like to ban novels, and moreover, to take aside their authors and throw them from clifftops into the ravine. *Men who write novels cannot be trusted*, they say. *In fact, plays and poems are just as bad. Though art never built a railway, or ploughed a field, artists are dangerous. We need more clifftops*, they say. It is the ability to complete and file one's own tax return, and by equal turns, the widespread availability of blank till receipts, that may upskill the work force. A man granted the authority and leave to hold weekly markets in the town square may demand two such days be tax free (specifically the feast days of St Augustine of Hippo, and St Basil Fool for Christ), or extract inflated fees with menaces because he doesn't give a shit about maintaining important social ties between urban and rural communities. Two men granted the authority and leave to hold weekly markets in the town square may happily collect all the booth fees themselves, or ask for a hint as to the true identity of he who wanders the market in long black cloak and hood and to whom all the market stall holders give freely of their goods and services. He who wears the long black cloak and hood is not a ghost, but he haunts the men's thoughts and feelings, to the point whereby they can no longer enjoy their weekly markets, nor the vast sums of money they earn from them.

Finola Scott

MOSS

a word sometimes used to describe a raised peat bog. Formally meaning a simple plant life, usually found in wet areas. Considered a nuisance by most, flowerless, its velvet cloaks harsh stone, dulls granite's cheer, delves deep in crannies. Silent it offers shelter to insect communities, has a life of its own. As in that soft green of my father's eyes glimpsed when he made his face naked to wash. As in the coast of Eire as the boat slid away, Dad humming an air. Off key. As in all-day ladder-scaling to clear moss, the song of the bath-soaked father. As in the shade and stitch of knitting favoured by aunts. Hunched over my Science homework, eyes strained from studying invertebrates I'd pull a cardigan close. Such tiny creatures which tremble and scurry as we scour between paving stones.

The word creeps into towns, marks those unfit places, spongy, unreliable. Spaces to edge round, hesitant as when watching eggs hatch. Beaks hacking shells. Feathers unsticking imperceptibly. As in the time you held graying bones, sponge-weightless, littered on to the greening patio. Tumbled into that emerald pile, its soft way smoothing edges. Into harlequin mosses that branch freely into microscopic chaos. Like early pioneers, these mosses set off singing.

Oft times associated with constant instability although its movements seem infinitesimal, unmeasurable. Like envy, it edges discretely, a man in a city suit, cuff-linked, brief-cased, trustworthy until it becomes a problem. As in moorland, a wide bare expanse offering no shelter. Where bog cotton shivers in summer heat and sphagnum colonises north-facing trunks of trees. As in guiding the lost traveller home to safety.

Elissa Soave

BLOOD

They sit on the hard chairs outside the head teacher's office, Liam reassuring Bernadette with a smile just wide enough to cause his eyes to wrinkle at the edges. He thinks she doesn't notice that his hands are balled into fists.

'Smells like our old school,' says Bernadette, looking around at the bright blue and yellow walls, and smelling the mingled aromas of bleach, fried food and soiled underwear from the nursery classes.

'You say that every time we're here,' says Liam.

He looks over at the children smiling back at him from the Achievements Wall, clutching their dance trophies and certificates for swimming fifty metres back crawl. Jack does not have his picture on the wall.

'You're right though. Some things never change,' he says, touching her knee. He draws his hand away quickly as the office door opens and the school secretary tells them the head teacher will see them shortly, thanks for their patience. They know it must be bad by the way she avoids looking at them when she closes the door behind her.

Bernie sighs softly, the way she does when she doesn't have the words, when what she feels about Jack wells up inside her and stops the words coming out. Her face is pale and angular, like that of a geisha, except that her eyes are an unexpected forget-me-not blue. The blue of their eyes is the only tell, Liam sometimes says at night, searching hers when they lie close and breathe in the other's breath.

'We'll be home soon,' he says. 'Whatever they tell us, whatever it is, we'll take him home with us now, get a hot chocolate maybe.'

'The flat will be cold,' says Bernie.

They've been in the current flat for six weeks, and are almost at the point where it feels familiar enough to be called home. Jack has his own room for the first time and though they worry about what he is doing in there when he closes his door each evening, they are pleased they can give him a room of his own. It is one of the reasons they love their little flat, the fourth they have lived in in the last year.

None of the flats are like the house they grew up in. Low-slung with a honeycomb of windows, the crumbling building would have been enough to satisfy even the most demanding imagination; its location at the edge of thick woods, which were sliced through with the murky Clyde, raised it to a child's paradise.

As children, Liam and Bernie cycled through the sweet-smelling trees, their wheels getting caught in the musty undergrowth and tripping them up. They mashed up rose petals that were strewn over the paths and Father Boyce let them set up a makeshift stand where they could sell petal perfume to villagers after Mass on Sundays. They disappeared for a day at a time, with their jam sandwiches and plastic bottles filled with tap water.

Swimming in the river every day, their little bodies were lean and uncomplicated. The water was often scummy and their feet would scrape against bottle tops and worse, thrown in unseen by the older kids who came to the river at night, long after Liam and Bernie had gone home. During the day though, they saw no-one at their spot beside the old tyre swing. For a few weeks each summer, it was hot enough to swim naked.

One August, Liam remembers, Bernie's school friend Louise came to stay while her mother was working. She didn't stay long, complaining that Liam and Bernie were leaving her out, with their secret language and the way each always knew what the other was thinking, the way they always agreed with each other, and laughed together, heads close. 'Tell *me*,' Louise would say, whining and curling her hair round her finger. 'Let me play.' 'What are you doing?' 'Let *me* see.' Finally, she'd given up trying to edge her way in and asked to be taken home early. Her mother had narrowed her eyes at Liam and Bernie and told Liam he should be spending time with boys his own age, instead of hanging around with the girls.

When they were older, they swam to reward themselves after a day's studying, luxuriating in the cool water that soothed their cramped limbs. That first time, they were late to the river because Liam had been studying for a physics exam. It was dusk, too cold to swim really. Bernie's skin was covered in gooseflesh, bumps appearing like molluscum on her smooth stomach and down the edges of her thighs. She ran into the water, laughing and breathless with the cold, shouting at him to hurry up. He called to her to wait on him, his voice breaking as he shouted after her, and she teased him for the occasional high note mingled with the gruffness. She slipped on the mossy floor of the river and he gripped her by her elbow, holding her there for a long time before passing the palm of his hand up towards the bumpy flesh of her cold upper arm. He carried on kneading her skin long after she regained her balance, slowly warming her. Black shadows and the slow lapping of the waves enveloped them, their desire a frightened thing, but determined to claw its way out. They stood knee deep in the water, entwined ropes of bone and muscle and skin, gelled by blood. They laid each other bare.

Later, when asked what they'd been up to, and whether they'd been swimming further out than they should, they shook their heads. It was clear something was different but nobody guessed they had become secret-keepers. After Mass the following Sunday, Father Boyce commented on how well they looked, how grown-up they were becoming. If he noticed they no longer attended Confession, he kept quiet on the matter.

At seventeen, drained and tired of hiding, Liam had gone away to uni. They coped without each other for weeks at a time then

Bernie would write him a letter that set him on fire, and he could not resist. It seemed that love – fine-grained and complex sexual love – was an enemy submarine that could surface anywhere. They surrendered to it and sometimes, revelled in it.

Just the one child, she said, after they had both graduated and home was far away. It had become an obsession – she'd watch the children being pushed around in their prams like little Prussian aristocrats, their blonde bobs shimmering. Liam thought it'd be pushing their luck but she'd read the statistics – there was a greater chance of being injured by a rocket on its way to the moon than their conceiving a damaged child. She said these things with a straight face, but she said them at the right times, when she knew he could not refuse her.

Sitting now outside the head teacher's office, Liam reflects that he cannot remember a time when Jack was not in trouble. He started with tantrums and screaming and has worked his way up to playground fights, behaviour charts, and being a permanent fixture outside the head teacher's office. It isn't always others he hurts – last year he stole Miss McAuliffe's special sharp scissors and sliced the top off his own thumb, clean through like an onion. Before the teacher could stop him, he'd popped the little chunk of soft flesh into his mouth and swallowed it, dark blood trailing down his chin like melted chocolate. When they got back from the hospital and put him to bed, Bernie cried so hard Liam was worried she would damage her beautiful blue eyes. He lay close to her and let her feel the weight of him, pushing strands of wet hair away from her face and whispering he'd never let her go.

At home, Jack rarely speaks. At breakfast, he points to the milk and Bernie pours it on his cereal; he completes his homework silently; and goes to bed without saying goodnight to either of his parents. His silence is amplified in the small flat, swirling around in the murk of his parents' desire and guilt, and meshing with the silence and secrets which surround their flawed love.

The door opens again and the school secretary ushers them through to the inner office. Mrs Miller does not look up as they enter. She carries on typing on her keyboard, her eyes moving slowly across the screen in time to her tapping.

Liam and Bernie take a seat, Bernie sitting on her hands. Liam can see the faint blue vein pulsating at the side of her eye.

'Now then, Mr and Mrs . . .'

'It's Liam and Bernadette. We are not . . .'

'Quite. Well, here we are again.' The head teacher taps her fingers on the desk. They listen as she tells them how they managed to stop Jack from cutting a little girl's wrist, though he had already cut his own in preparation. They nod as she tells them he is not a bad boy, but he is troubled. More troubled than they can help him with at this school. They say nothing as she says, in the tone she reserves for her most difficult pupils, the one that brooks no argument, that the time has come for them to consider another school for their son.

*

They sit in their green Fiesta, staring straight ahead. Jack is in the back seat, headphones over his ears and eyes glued to the screen of his iPad. His feet bash rhythmically against the back of Bernie's seat but she says nothing.

'Okay,' says Liam, eyeing Jack to make sure he is not listening. 'It's not the end of the world. We'll talk to him at home, make him see he can't carry on like this.'

'What about schools? Where's he going to go?'

'We could stay in the village and try the new school. The one by the library, it's not that much further.'

Bernadette swings round in her seat and says, 'The Proddy . . . Protestant school? Oh Liam, we can't send him there.'

'Bernie, come on, we're not in any position to pick and choose. Anyway, it's non-denominational, not Protestant. We'll still take him to Mass, teach him what's right.'

He looks at Bernie and sees the flush of her cheeks and her eyelids begin to redden.

'Don't cry Bernie, please. Not in front of Jack.' He turns round again but the child is oblivious to the world outside his iPad.

'This is our punishment, isn't it?' says Bernie. 'This is the price we've to pay.'

'That's bullshit, Bernie and you know it. He doesn't work that way.'

'No, it was fine, we were managing till we had Jack.' She lowers her voice unnecessarily. 'Till I insisted on having him.'

'Well, now we do have him and we love him and we wouldn't change that would we?'

Bernie doesn't answer.

'Remember we used to swim in the river, for hours sometimes, till we were so cold we couldn't even put our clothes back on. Our fingers refused to bend, remember, they were frozen solid. Remember Liam? When all we had to worry about was . . . nobody seeing us. No-one knew, not a thing. We were so happy, weren't we Liam?'

Liam squeezes her hand.

'I remember,' he says. He looks away for a moment then back at Bernie as he says, 'Listen, we might have to leave anyway. I saw Father Boyce this morning, coming out of the library. He said he's covering at St John's till Father Leary gets better.'

'Liam, why did you not tell me? What did he say?'

'He said he was sorry to hear about Mum passing away. He asked after you. I told him I hadn't seen you in a while—'

'But Liam, that was the worst thing to say. Now what if he bumps into me?'

'I never thought . . .'

A man in a flat cap, walking a pair of clumsy black Labradors, passes in front of their car. They watch the dogs lumbering across the road, nosing each other and getting in the man's way. Ahead, the traffic lights change to green and cars swing by, taking their passengers home to family dinners and TV and conversations about their day.

Liam turns the key in the ignition and the car's engine starts to rumble. He reaches across Bernie, finds her seatbelt and straps her in. She is biting the edge of her thumbnail the way she's done for as long as Liam can remember.

'We'll pack the car in the morning,' he says, gently taking her thumb away from her mouth and holding her hand in his. 'Maybe try further up north. It'll be an adventure for Jack. For the whole family.'

Dan Spencer

OUR COMMON AREAS

Yesterday evening we were without apologies or absences. Everyone was present, which is to say that everyone was represented: all of the homes in 55 as well as the private entrances – 56, 56B (the garden flat) and 54 (the duplex). Certainly, not every single body was with us at the kitchen table of 1/1. There were those members of couples who might sometimes be here or sometimes not, sometimes one, sometimes the other. There were also, on various floors of the building, three dogs locked away, each awaiting its master's return, watching the front door, watching the ceiling, padding through every room of their home, one room after the other, in a circuit, again and again. As well as this, in two different flats, a total of four children were sleeping or should have been sleeping, and their quiet, housewifey fathers were watching over them while their wives, with us here, sipped prosecco and dealt with the matters at hand. Or, otherwise, we were sole occupants, we lived alone, and when we left our homes, day or night, we left them empty.

We're a marvellous assortment of characters, it has to be said – the short-haul pilot (2/2), the mathematics lecturer (2/1), the security entrepreneur (the Duplex) – quite the 'cave of wonders', and all homeowners, crucially, so we're invested in the upkeep. All agree that it's lucky we price out the students, though we're grateful for our old and noteworthy university and all it brings us, the enlightened progress, the economic gains, the well-mannered lodgers . . . and if any development on campus might help or hinder us, the mathematics lecturer will always have the inside scoop. We're all of us useful, to each other, to the building. The Duplex, for example, has rigged out everywhere with the finest security system. We know basic plumbing. We grow vegetables. We're almost self-sufficient. We're a village. If we hear it said how like the cast of *44 Scotland Street* we are, we take it in good humour (though of course you'd have the city wrong). What's more, we're interested in one another 'as people', even if we don't show it. We care about each other, as much as one ought. It would be preferable to ask after the husbands and children. It would be preferable to ask after the Duplex's wife. But there's so much before this that must be discussed.

We must address 2/2's ceiling, which leaks and is thus everybody's leak. We must address the Garden Flat's floor, which floods so is everybody's flood. We must address the maintenance of all our common areas: the scattered pine needles left unswept on the stairs for at least two hours on New Year's morning, the festivities long finished with; the rainbow chalk drawings of horses and fish remaining for over a day on the garden path (but which I didn't mind washing away myself, and for which I don't expect thanks). Reminders about entranceways are necessary, too, because the back gate has been left unlatched, again and again, and the front door not pulled shut, repeatedly, despite the reminders, despite the little notices I put on labels and stick to the wooden post, these labels remaining there, clear as day, for weeks, until they fade out in the sun.

Truth be told, not everyone is always 'in line'. We aren't always 'of one purpose'. It wasn't obvious that everybody wanted the same thing from last night's meeting. To begin with, 2/2 turned up with his partner Stevie (the boy), which already gave 2/2 'too many votes', but then he said, 'And this is Stevie's pal, who'll be taking the minutes.' General response to this was that we didn't need minutes, let alone a minute-taker, so Stevie's friend was ushered out, and Stevie too. ('No, please don't wait in the living room, Stevie. Wouldn't you be more comfortable back in your own home?') Minutes! We all have good memories, don't we, however advanced in years we've become? Minutes! He hadn't even brought a pen and paper. They were undoubtedly here more than anything else for the prosecco, a little too much of which flowed. Is it indecorous to add that Stevie appears to be only an occasional fixture? Can Stevie really be called a resident? Is he, in any sense, a 'homeowner', and if not, is he due a say? The point is, the *key* is, does he really care as we care, as profoundly as we care, for the building?

That awkwardness over and done with, we had a full agenda and not a second more to enquire about Stevie or Stevie's friend or about where Stevie goes when he's gone. There was no time, either, to enquire about the nervous husbands who flee from you, mumbling and frowning, whenever you stumble upon them, or to ask after the little children who admittedly are inevitable and somewhat necessary in all this, because a cultivated garden must, too some extent, be 'enjoyed' by someone. Nor was there any time to ask about the Duplex's somewhat young and carefully shaped wife who was known, some afternoons, to teach handstands at the art cooperative and who was overheard in the porch last month, the other side of the door, berating our hanging baskets, very worked up, as if her upset was really about more than just hanging baskets, which are just hanging baskets, after all, though there is certainly a right sort of hanging basket and a wrong sort of hanging basket, but if anyone was putting too much emotion into the hanging baskets it was her, the Duplex's wife, and no one else, and if this was the last straw, what were the other straws, and if she didn't value all our friendly rules and regulations, would she rather live somewhere they shit in the stairwell and shoot-up in the street?

It's not lack of concern, but because we have the good grace not to ask. It's not that we don't care, but because it makes no difference (thinking beyond ourselves, thinking of the building) whether the Duplex is with or without a wife.

Our final item was the trespass. While we reclined a little drunkenly in the antique farmhouse chairs of the 1/1 kitchen, 1/2 recounted, like a fireside tale, how her husband, entering their study at dusk, had heard voices under their window and discovered, below, the boys, sitting out on the patio of the Garden Flat, rolling-up at the table outside the Garden Flat's door. Were they cigarettes? We mightn't have minded (somebody said), if they were only cigarettes. But there's a drug problem in the park at night, not to mention a drink problem, a refuse problem and therefore a rat problem, a noise problem, a problem with homelessness, a youth problem, a problem with gentrification and tourism and an immigration problem, a problem with the gangs of lazy, drug-taking refuse workers, a problem with the students, also in gangs, also lazy, also drunken and on drugs. Even here, crime enters: last month, a woman robbed at knifepoint. 'Could the boys have been our neighbours?' we wondered. Once before, we called the police on our neighbours, mistaking them for interlopers. But everyone knows everyone now; and those neighbours, they didn't really fit in, they didn't last long.

Unchecked, our discussion of the trespass found no solution that night, sliding instead into a debate on the idea of 'property' and how, in an ideal world, no one would own anything, about the far-reaching influence of the idea of 'mine' and 'yours' and the impossibility of ideals, and isn't it edifying to be in such company, to identify and see eye-to-eye with all these other minds all under the same roof as you, to be all of this one stratum by virtue of our educations and our incomes and our aspirations? Granted, 'property' might be undesirable, in a perfect world, but how good to share this property with them. Granted, 'us and them' might be a bad idea, but if there wasn't a 'them', there couldn't be an 'us', and how good it is to be us.

That night, I slept deeply, having drunk too much sparkling wine, and seeming to hear, as I drifted off, a piano playing somewhere in the building, and finding the last thoughts of the day that wandered into my fading awareness to be a question about who was playing, about from which floor and from which home the music floated, because so many of us own pianos, so many of us play. 'By my count, five pianos surround you,' the warm thought said, as I fell into slumber, filled with happiness whether or not I truly, at that moment, heard any music play.

But, tonight, I can't forget the trespass. I can't get comfortable. Outside, a car alarm is going and I'm thinking about all the other bodies in this building, if they hear it. I'm thinking of the Duplex below me, alone in his bed and if he hears the car alarm, or if he sleeps as the car alarm sounds and sounds, dreaming of the wife and daughter who used to live with him until they slipped away, the wife and daughter whom he secured for a while but only, as with any owned thing, for a while.

Iain Twiddy

MAYBE

maybe
if rivastigmine (Exelon) was switched with donepezil
(Aricept), i.e. $C_{14}H_{22}N_2O_2$
swopped for (swapped for) $C_{24}H_{29}NO_3$, or at least for
three months, just to
see if there was any correlation
or if she'd ever felt comfortable swimming with her head
underwater
or if her favourite perfume hadn't been the fresh of Chanel
No. 5, but Arpège
or if she'd had her last baby at 39 years and 364 days, not 40
years and 16 days
or if she hadn't had her gall bladder taken out when I was
three, and could have
eaten cream, and I hadn't pissed on the floor of the
train when
Grandma took me and my brother to visit her
or if she hadn't retired early due to the stress of more
frequent evidence in court, I
mean, really, it seemed to be every other week, and
everything had to be
computerised, it would be taking her ages to write up
her notes
or if she'd come sledging with us at Ancaster Valley one of
the fantastic handful
of days it snowed between 1979 and 1990
or if she'd walked for two miles three times a week during
her forties
or if there was a clear way to tell whether it was proteins
depositing in nerve

cells, a bit like a river silting a slip-off slope, blocking the flow of
messages, or is it messengers, especially acetylcholine and dopamine, if
there was a way to sweep that away, or if it's the vessels themselves
droughting out, solidifying at the spring, leaving whole regions of the
brain cut off like ox-bow lakes, leaving her stranded from the stream of
understanding
or if she'd done an evening class when she finished work, *Introductory Spanish,*
Excel for Beginners, something like that
or if she'd ever really been bothered about dusting, because she wasn't, in all
honesty, I mean, I feel the same way, what is the point, really, you can
never be clear of the sense that everything falls apart
or if she'd eaten a steak-and-ale pie instead of Roast Beef and Yorkshire Pudding
and All the Trimming's on Sunday, November 20th, 1983
or if she and my dad had been to France on a summer holiday before we were
born, seen the delicious dazzle left by the sea on the causeway out to
Mont St Michel
or if she'd eaten more nuts (particularly walnuts), other than just a handful of

hazelnuts at Christmas
or if they'd lived in a bigger town, or a village, or a city, if they'd moved back to
where they were born
or if she'd never felt nervous – blood-drumming terrified – speaking in front of
people, even something simple, like a reading in church
or if she hadn't had breast cancer, had the laser zapping at her for so many
weeks
or if she hadn't always preferred her hair short, always short, because it was
easier to take care of
or if she'd drunk more alcohol than just a few glasses of wine with dinner on
Saturday night to lower the blood pressure, push back the tide of
diabetes
or if she'd walked for three miles twice a week during her forties
or if the Conservatives hadn't closed the lab where my dad happily worked
or if she hadn't read *Excellent Women* more than ten times, but something else
or more
or more
or more
or more

maybe this wouldn't have come to grief
like a brain wave never reaching shore
maybe the brain wouldn't be shore
worn away by its waves

Lois Wappler

BLETHER

There's a coarseness ti it that disnae
suit a wummin. It's a grunny voice
that wints a man ti spik it.

An fit why? Av nae ony less claim ti
th north sea's gripe an th dreech
throat that gies it breath. Th midwifie
cry'd me *quine*, no girl. A quine's a
quine fir a that, tae.

Some spiel noo about hoo it's nae seemly.
Wummin are there ti be understood
or some ither blether. Aye? Am nae
handin masel back ti that yoke.

We learnt aff th boats same as yous menfolk,
we jist werna sailin. Reekin o yer fish an
yer broth and the soap fur yer breeks. Hauns as
rough as th patter. Nae seemly ma erse.

Fan I hae ma bairns – an bairns they'll be –
I'll tell them a this an gie them the spik.
Wur nae learnt o'er the herrin guts ti cast
oorsels awa wi that muck.

Lynnda Wardle

THE FIGHT

Joburg Saturdays are listless and hot, filled with the sound of Mr Baxter next door fixing his car, clattering spanners on the driveway to the pitch and roar of the rugby commentary flowing over the fence. Sometimes he sings loudly and sometimes he swears when something goes wrong. 'Honestly,' my mother says, banging the window shut, trapping hot air and flies inside to keep his bad language out.

But Saturday the First of December 1973 is different. We are fizzing with the news that tonight the Big Fight is happening at the Rand Stadium. My father says we'll listen to it on the radio because the tickets are too expensive, but Russel Peach and Gavin Khoury in my class are going.

'Girls can't go to the boxing,' Gavin says when I ask how much their tickets cost. 'And anyway, you don't even know what light-heavyweight is.'

'I do know,' I snap back but have to ask my father when I get home to make sure I don't get caught out like that again.

This will be the fight to end all fights: South Africa's Pierre Fourie is fighting America's Bob Foster, and it's the first time a black man has fought a white man in the professional ring in South Africa. *The blood is going to flow, just you watch!* The boys are shadow boxing, throwing punches and going crazy. The whole school has been in an uproar all week. 'It'll be a knockout, ja, well maybe. Last time they fought, Foster won on points, but Piri is strong! He'll just knock him flat one time.'

We throw hooks left and right, dance on the balls of our feet and fall to the ground, legs splayed and eyes rolling to show that this is a knock out. *Piri, Piri, Piri* we chant.

'I hope he moers the af,' says Colin Sharp and I am shocked at how bad this sounds out loud, even though this is really what all the high jinks and sharp upper cuts are about. It's about 'We'll show Them.' We'll show Them who's the baas of the plaas here in South Africa; home of braaivleis, rugby, sunny skies and the great white hope Piri Fourie who looks like he's walked straight out of a Western with his curly moustache and slow sneer.

'He's a handsome chappie for a boxer. I like his style,' says my mother who usually pays no attention to sport, especially boxing.

My father is proud that we have allowed Bob Foster into our country. 'It's not like he's any native boy; he's a professional,' he explains to me. Piet Koornhorf, the sad-eyed minister of Home Affairs has wangled a proclamation, a ministerial declaration to change the ban on interracial sport, just this once, so that we can all enjoy seeing our Piri Fourie finish off that Bob Foster. It's blood-tingling stuff – in the heat of a summer's night two men bobbing and weaving, throwing a jab and cross, a sharp uppercut to the jaw and then the magnificent topple of a man down.

I can't wait.

We'll listen to the fight on the radio. My father wipes down the wireless with his car chammy and places it in the centre of the kitchen table. My mother is irritated at being chased out of her kitchen. 'It's *Pierre* Fourie,' she says to me, 'not Piri.' But I don't care: Piri sounds better than oo-la-la Pierre Fourie. *Piri! Piri! Piri!* I squeal, dancing from one leg to the other until she tells me shush, she can't hear herself think.

It's dark by the time the fight starts. The Toweel brothers who organised the fight are interviewed on Springbok Radio. We eat peanuts and crisps and my father has a couple of Castle lagers lined up so that he won't miss any of the action. The bell clangs to start the fight and every time Piri strikes a blow, the crowd roars. Round after furious round, the gloves slap, the boxers grunt, the crowd yells with excitement. Piri slumps exhausted against the ropes but heaves himself into the ring once again. Our hearts swell and dip as Piri slugs his way through each round, blow by blow to the bitter end. But it was never meant to be, and too soon it is over.

I can't believe it. We've lost.

'We lost on points,' my father explains to me, but losing is losing. Piri is sweaty and bloodied and the next day I see photos from the fight in *The Sunday Times*: Bob Foster holds his gloved fists high in the air.

At school we discuss the fight in an off-hand, subdued kind of way. Ja, it was a good fight and Piri really pulled out all the stops. But Bob Foster was just bigger and had more experience. Piri was never going to win, was he?

And then as soon as we can, we stop talking about the fight and move onto other things. Although I am only ten, I have an instinct that what has happened in the ring at the Rand Stadium is bigger than two men battering each other until one of them wins. This fight is the first time that whites and blacks were able to buy tickets to attend the same sporting event – a racially mixed crowd of thirty-eight thousand seated together in a country where we are separated in everything else.

When Fourie lost, as disappointing as that was for organisers and fans, the profits from the match were a comfort, and a precedent was set. Those who predicted trouble on the night were proved wrong. Perhaps blacks and whites were cheering different men in that fight, but they managed to do this side by side, without the usual racial animosity that was part of everyday South African life. 'Mixed bouts' were later legalised in 1977 and in 1979 the system of 'white' and 'supreme' titles was discarded completely in South African boxing. Sport was becoming a way for a nation to express itself, its defiance and hopes born blow by blow in a boxing ring. The international sporting boycott was still in place and would stay in force for many years to come, but this match marked a relaxation of the rules for pleasure and for profit. It showed that it was possible for interracial sport to draw crowds, make money and provide entertainment for everyone, irrespective of the skin colour of the winner.

My father and I, sitting close to the radio, disappointed at the defeat of our hero Pierre Fourie that night, could have had no idea that this match marked a moment when the architecture of apartheid shifted and creaked. True, it was a small shift, but ultimately the distance we travelled as a nation in those fifteen bloody rounds in 1973 was more than the victory of Foster over Fourie; it was the harbinger of a future that was already being dreamed of and fought for across the land – a sign; bloodied, bruised and important, of a different way that we might live together.

Helen Welsh

FAIRY FAY

Jeanie's up the town, in Oxfam. She wants a new coat. The one she's wearing is too thin; her bronchitis is starting up already and it's only November.

This one would be warm, but too easily dirtied. No. This one reminds her of her mother. No. This one has fine big pockets, and she's tempted, but it wouldn't keep the cold out enough. No. She might give up and try Cancer Research up the road, but it's getting dark, nearly five o'clock, the shops are all shutting. She's not spending one more night in this too-thin coat.

The assistant looks at her with narrow eyes: 'We're shutting in five minutes,' she warns. Jeanie ignores her and keeps rifling along the rail. This one? Too wee. This one? Too big. This one? Cherry-red, soft and light. Four pounds. She starts unbuttoning her too-thin coat and the assistant snaps, 'you can't try it on!'

Other people get to try things on, thinks Jeanie. She knows the assistant's just worried that the smell of Jeanie will be passed on to the smell of other people's cast-offs. She sticks her nose in the air and drops the coat on the floor. She hobbles to the door; the rain has started again, sleety now. She gazes at the sleety High Street for a second, and changes her mind.

'We're closed!' shrieks the assistant. She has pulled the blinds and let the other volunteers out the side door. Jeanie starts unbuttoning her coat again. 'Stop that!' shouts the assistant. 'Leave right now!' She grips the cherry-red coat with white fingers.

Jeanie ignores her; finishes taking off her too-thin coat; gets her purse out; folds up her old coat and squeezes it into her bag; takes £4.50 out of her purse and drops it on the counter. 'That's fifty pee for the charity box,' she says, and takes the crimson cosy right out of the assistant's clutches. Light as a feather. Pure new wool! Worn around the collar and pockets of course. Jeanie shrugs herself into her new coat. Lovely. Top button missing, but her scarf will hide it.

The assistant is holding the door open: 'If you don't leave right now I'm calling the police,' she utters. Jeanie picks up her bags again, arranges one over her new red pure-new-wool shoulder, puts her mittens on, and heads out into the night. The sleet has stopped, it's cold but she's cosy.

She stumps along the East Port and past the police station to the hostel, at the twilight end of the shoppers' car park. There's a queue for signing-in, but it's not too long; there are seven in front of her, the usual crowd apart from one woman she's never seen before. She's in plenty time to get a bed.

She hunkers down while the officers fill in the forms and search the bags. It's for everyone's protection. Aggie Wilson has her vodka confiscated, she should know better by now. They've got eyes in the back of their heads.

Eventually it's Jeanie's turn. She gets allocated a room and collects her bedroll. There's a tea trolley at half-past nine – nearly three hours to wait. She climbs the stairs to her cubicle on the second floor. She wonders who she's sharing with tonight, and soon finds out as the other occupant is already in place: it's the new one. Jeanie nods at her, and the other one says hello and tells Jeanie her name is Fay, as if Jeanie needs to know. 'What's yours?' Fay asks; but Jeanie has taken her mittens off and put her hands in her pockets. There's something crisp and rustly; she pulls it out. It's a tenner. She stares at it. 'Ooooh!' squeals Fay, 'you're rich!' Jeanie buttons up and puts her mittens back on. Fay says, 'You're going back out?' which is a bit obvious, thinks Jeanie, even she could have worked that one out. 'Where are you going?' asks Fay. Nosey, like.

'The police station.'

'The police station?' Slow on the uptake. 'What for?'

'Because Oxfam's shut now.' And off she goes.

She gets lucky. The desk sergeant on duty is Willie McFarlane, they go back a long way. Jeanie knew his mother. Willie gives her a coffee, two sugars, from the staff canteen vending machine and Jeanie gives him the tenner.

'Probably nobody will claim it,' he says. Jeanie shrugs. 'Why not just tuck it in your purse? Buy yourself a fish supper on your way up the road?' But he knows her views on theft. If it's not been claimed in three months' time she'll get it back anyway. That's different.

Back at the hostel, Jeanie sits in the TV room and waits for the trolley to appear. Fay comes in and sits down beside her. 'Did you get to the police station?' she asks. Jeanie nods. 'You should get a reward.' Jeanie grunts. 'Tell you what,' Fay whispers, leaning forward, 'I'll give you a reward myself, because you deserve one, being honest like that.' Jeanie looks at her; what's she on about now?

Fay's eyes are shining. Has she taken something, Jeanie wonders? Better not let the officers find out. Fay leans further into Jeanie. 'I will grant you three wishes!' she breathes, and Jeanie is surprised at that. She thought fairies died young, and this one was sixty if she was a day. Maybe fifty if she's a drinker; and she must be, or she wouldn't be in this place.

'Go on,' Fay urges. 'What three things would you most like in the whole wide world? Just name them and they're yours.'

Jeanie gives it some thought.

'Well?' Fay prompts.

Jeanie gives it some more thought.

'Come on,' says Fay.

'It would be a fine thing to have my bunions done,' says Jeanie.

'Your bunions? What a waste of a wish! I could give you a gold-plated chauffeur-driven Rolls-Royce if you wanted to spare your feet.'

'No, I don't trust chauffeurs. My feet are giving me gyp.'

'Okay,' Fay sighs, 'I'll sort it out. Wish number two?'

Jeanie thinks again. 'Credit at Karla's Kaff,' she says. 'I'll pay it back when I can, but I hate those cold days whey you're just tuppence short of a mutton pie.'

'A mutton pie . . . What's wrong with roast chicken and all the trimmings? Strawberries and cream? Pepperoni pizza?'

Jeanie gives this some consideration. 'I like a good mutton pie,' she says. 'Maybe with some mushy peas.'

Fay sighs again. 'Okay, credit at Karla's Kaff. What about your third and final wish? Be careful with this one, it's the most important.'

Jeanie thinks carefully. Fay can't wait; too impatient. 'For instance,' she urges, 'many of my clients wish for eternal youth.' Oh yeah? 'Or great beauty.' Uh-huh. Overrated, in Jeanie's book. 'Or a nice new Barratt bungalow, with the gas and electricity paid for life.'

Got it. 'What I want,' says Jeanie, 'is a guaranteed bed here every night, and not have them forever hassling me to get my own flat.'

Fay's face falls. 'Is that really it?' she asks. 'You're not very ambitious, are you?' That's true, thinks Jeanie. 'Oh all right,' says Fay. 'When you wake up in the morning you'll have your wishes.' The officers come in with their kettles and teabags, and Jeanie gets up to join the queue. 'Tell you what,' says Fay, catching Jeanie's arm. 'You can have a bonus wish too, for later. Since you might wish you'd chosen better. You have to use it within twenty-four hours though.' Jeanie nods and holds out her mug to the officer.

The following day is full of surprises. Three, to be precise.

First, as Jeanie is eating her cornflakes, the officers bring in the mail and there's a letter for Jeanie. She'd forgotten she'd given this address. From the hospital – an appointment in a week's time to get her bunions done.

Second, as she's signing out, the senior officer calls her into the office and tells Jeanie they've had a meeting. 'You're not really ready to put down roots, Jeanie, are you?' she says, and Jeanie just looks at her. 'I mean, we counted it up and realised you've had sixteen shots at rehousing.' Jeanie nods. 'You don't really want your own place, do you?' Jeanie shakes her head. 'Well, it's against policy, but we're making a special case for you,' says the officer. 'Don't go telling everybody, but so long as you're dry and stay out of trouble, there'll be a bed here for you every night.' Well! Jeanie feels as if she's won the lottery.

She goes out for her morning walk. Her feet are killing her – but only for another week. She thinks about Fay. Who would have thought? Jeanie never took her for a fairy.

Having bought the coat, Jeanie doesn't have enough left for a mutton pie, but decides to go to Karla's anyway, in by the bus station, for a cup of tea. Karla is at the stove herself – she must have sacked that idle son of hers. 'Mutton pie, Jeanie?' she asks. 'I kept you one.' Jeanie gesticulates limply; Karla understands straight away. 'I'll put it on the slate,' she says, and ladles a big spoonful of steaming mushy peas and a pool of gravy on top of Jeanie's pie. Jeanie thinks if she's not careful she might shed a tear. She wonders if Fay will be back at the hostel tonight; she'll need to do something nice for her.

No sign of Fay in the queue, and they're keeping everyone waiting outside in the cold. There's shouting above, and all the women look up. There's Fay standing on the very top windowledge – waving her arms about, quite reckless-like. One of the officers is at the next window, reaching out; the other is down on the ground, shouting. A police car shoots into the street, blue lights flashing but no siren; Willie McFarlane and a policewoman. They can all hear Fay shouting, 'I can fly! I can fly!' They're having the Dickens of a job trying to stop her. She'll be dead in an instant.

Jeanie hugs her new red coat about her. She remembers her bonus wish. She closes her eyes and wishes it. Hard. When she opens them again and looks up, Fay's not there. Jeanie looks down, one eye closed just in case. Fay's not there either. Jeanie looks back up. Fay's taken off. Fluttering, falling a bit, fluttering again, then up and away. That's good. That's good.

Mary Wight

3-2=1

—Encountering Salomon de Bray's* The Twins, *Scottish National Gallery

Two wee peas podded in shell, being borne
away farther than the frame allows us
to go, stare beyond each other, beyond
us all, pink cheeks greying, unwatched even
by the cherub lounging in a corner
grinning, perhaps because it isn't him
a-slosh in that gilded bed, so pretty
yet also shallow, it lets memory
trickle in . . . it's more than fifty years now
since a child ran, banged a neighbour's door, saw
her mother lifted from a yellow pail,
two blooded shapes left darkly at its base.

Unsmiling cherub, the only child bore
witness, too young to know what she had lost.

BIOGRAPHIES

James Aitchison's most recent collection, *Learning How to Sing*, was published by Mica Press in 2018. His publications include *The Gates of Light*, *Foraging: New & Selected Poems*, *New Guide to Poetry and Poetics*, *The Golden Harvester: The Vision of Edwin Muir*, and the *Cassell Dictionary of English Grammar*.

A Scottish Book Trust New Writer's Awardee for 2016, **Karen Ashe** has been shortlisted in the Fish prize, Highly Commended and shortlisted in the Bridport Prize, and been published in *Mslexia* and *Gutter* magazines.

Originally from Glasgow, **Pamela Beasant** has lived in Stromness, Orkney, for many years. She has published poetry and non-fiction books, was the first George Mackay Brown Fellow in 2007, and has had scripts commissioned by the St Magnus International Festival, for whom she directs the Orkney Writers' Course.

Henry Bell lives on the Southside of Glasgow and edits *Gutter Magazine*. His poetry has been published widely, and he has edited books including *A Bird is Not a Stone*, a collection of contemporary Palestinian poetry. His biography of *John Maclean: Hero of Red Clydeside* was published in 2018. You can find out more at **henryjimbell.com** or **@henbell**.

Born in Sheffield, **Eloise Birtwhistle** has lived in Glasgow since 2012. As well as writing her own poetry, she is interested in creating inclusive spaces that encourage writing and community. Eloise is a teacher, workshop facilitator, and a Director of the non-profit organisation Uncovered Artistry.

Chris Boyland is based in Cumbernauld. His poems have been published in *404Ink*, *Northwords Now*, *PENning* and *The Poets'*

Republic, and anthologies such as *Aiblins: New Scottish Political Poetry*. He performs regularly at spoken word nights across Central Scotland and blogs occasionally at **www.theglasgowempire.scot**.

Sam Burns is a Cardiff-born playwright. Her first full-length play, *Not the Worst Place*, was produced by Paines Plough in April–May 2014. Her radio play *Floor 13* aired on BBC Radio 4's Afternoon Drama slot in late May 2017. She lives in Shetland.

Norman Coburn is a short story writer and novelist. An Ulsterman, living in the East Neuk of Fife, he beachcombs Scotland for mysteries and legends, stories to polish and embellish. He once met a guy who believed a unicorn killed his son, but that's another story for another day.

Krishan Coupland is a graduate from the University of East Anglia MA Creative Writing programme. His debut chapbook *When You Lived Inside The Walls* is available from Stonewood Press. He runs and edits *Neon Literary Magazine*. He is unduly preoccupied with theme parks. His website is **www.krishancoupland.co.uk**.

Anna Crowe is a co-founder of StAnza. Her translations from Catalan and Spanish (Bloodaxe and Arc) brought a Society of Authors Travelling Scholarship. Her poetry has been recorded for the Poetry Archive and awarded the Peterloo Prize, the Callum Macdonald Memorial Award, and two PBS Choices. Her third collection is due from Arc in September.

Alec Finlay (Scotland, 1966–) is an artist and poet whose work crosses over a range of media and forms.

Imogen Forster has worked as a teacher, a librarian and a translator from French, Spanish and Italian. She is currently learning

Catalan. She was one of two translators from French for the new edition of Van Gogh's letters, published by the Van Gogh Museum, Amsterdam. She has an MA in Writing Poetry from Newcastle University, and lives in Edinburgh. She tweets as **@ForsterImogen**.

Pippa Goldschmidt is the author of the novel *The Falling Sky* and the short story collection *The Need for Better Regulation of Outer Space*. Her work has been broadcast on Radio 4 and appeared in a variety of publications including *A Year of Scottish Poetry*, *Multiverse* and *Best American Science and Nature Writing 2014*.

Stephanie Green's most recent pamphlet is *Flout* (HappenStance, 2015). Her poetry was set to music by Marisa Sharon Hartanto at the St Magnus Festival, 2013, and inspired a dance choreographed by Mathew Hawkins, Edinburgh, 2015. 'Berlin Umbrella', a collaboration with Sound Artist, Sonja Heyer, launched in Berlin, 2018. **www.stephaniegreen.org.uk**

Lesley Harrison lives and works on the Angus coast. Her most recent collections are *Blue Pearl* (New Directions, 2017) and *Disappearance* (Shearsman, 2020). 'Eday, North Isles' was set to music by Alastair Matthews and performed at the Conservatoire, Valenciennes, France.

Izabela Ilowska holds a PhD in English Literature and Creative Writing from the University of Glasgow. She lives in Warsaw.

Published poet, fiction writer, playwright, **Anita John**'s work is printed in anthologies and magazines throughout Scotland, with work performed at TalkFest in the Borders, DunsPlayFest, and a Borders tour planned of her short play, 'First Steps', autumn 2019. She is also Writer in Residence for RSPB Scotland Loch Leven. **anitajohn.co.uk**

Shane Johnstone is a scriever in the Scots Language raised in Govanhill, Glasgow, an experience which influenced him profoundly. He spent his twenties working as a traditional musician/grafter of many hopeless jobs, before turning to writing. His prose has been published with *Lallans* and *Pushing Out the Boat* literary magazines.

Ingrid Leonard currently lives in London but comes from Orkney, a place which greatly influences her poetry. She graduated from Newcastle University in 2017 with an MA in Writing Poetry and is particularly interested in writing poetry in Orcadian. Her work has been published in *Brittle Star* and *Northwords Now*.

Shona McCombes is from Glasgow and currently lives in the Netherlands. She holds an MLitt in Modernities and an MA in Gender Studies. Her fiction and essays appear sporadically: in *3:AM*, *Gorse*, *Popula*, and the *Glasgow Review of Books*, and others.

Neil McCrindle lives in Edinburgh and does stuff. Also writes songs and occasionally performs as thepuregallus.

Stuart Macdonald has been published in a range of anthologies and magazines including *New Writing Scotland*, *Rialto*, *Other Poetry*, and *Acumen*. He works as a Digital Archivist and lives in Edinburgh with his wife and three children.

Crìsdean MacIlleBhàin / Christopher Whyte is a poet in Gaelic, a novelist in English, and the translator from Russian of the poetry of Marina Tsvetaeva (1892–1941). After teaching at the universities of Rome, Edinburgh and Glasgow, he moved in 2006 to Budapest where he writes full-time. His sixth collection *Ceum air cheum / Step by step*, with facing English translations by Niall O'Gallagher, is published by Acair in 2019.

Laura Muetzelfeldt has been published in journals such as *The International Literary Quarterly*, *Bandit Fiction*, and *Ink, Sweat and Tears*. She is a graduate of the University of Glasgow's Creative Writing MLitt and has been awarded a scholarship for a Creative Writing PhD at the University of St Andrews.

Colette O'Connor is a poet and aspiring therapist living in Glasgow. Her writing has featured in publications including *Gutter*, *MAP Magazine*, *From Glasgow to Saturn*, *Rose Quartz Magazine* and *SPAM*. Find her on Twitter **@MedusaDolorosa**.

Niall O'Gallagher was born in 1981. He is the author of two collections of poetry, *Beatha Ùr* (Clàr, 2013) and *Suain nan Trì Latha* (Clàr, 2016). A third is due in 2020. A journalist to trade, he is poetry editor of the Gaelic journal *STEALL*. In 2019 he was named Bàrd Baile Ghlaschu, Glasgow's first Gaelic laureate.

Pip Osmond-Williams moved to Glasgow in 2010 to study at the University of Glasgow. At present she is completing her PhD research, which focuses on love in the life and work of Edwin Morgan. Her poetry has been published in *From Glasgow to Saturn*. She currently resides in Shawlands.

Alycia Pirmohamed is a PhD student at the University of Edinburgh and holds an MFA from the University of Oregon. She is the author of the chapbook *Faces that Fled the Wind* (BOAAT Press) and a recipient of a Literature Matters award from The Royal Society of Literature.

Martin Raymond has just completed the MLitt course in Creative Writing at Stirling University. Previously he has been involved in less creative forms of writing, working as a communication professional for the NHS, various universities, the BBC and his own company Cloudline. He lives in Milnathort.

Calum Rodger is a Glasgow-based poet and researcher, and current (2019) Scottish National Slam Champion. His publications include *Know Yr Stuff: Poems on Hedonism* (Tapsalteerie) and *PORTS* (SPAM Press), and his next pamphlet, *Rock, Star, North* – a poetic travelogue set in the *Grand Theft Auto* universe – is forthcoming from Tapsalteerie.

Cynthia Rogerson's work includes five novels and a collection of stories. *I Love You Goodbye* was translated into six languages, shortlisted for Novel of the Year, and dramatised for BBC radio. Winner of the V. S. Pritchett Prize, her short stories have been widely anthologised. *Wait for Me Jack* is written under Addison Jones.

Mark Russell's full collections are *Spearmint & Rescue* (Pindrop), and *Shopping for Punks* (Hesterglock). The poem here is from a new collection, *Men Who Repeat Themselves.* Other poems have appeared in *Shearsman, Stand, Tears in the Fence, The Scores, Blackbox Manifold, The Lonely Crowd, Molly Bloom*, and elsewhere.

This year **Finola Scott** won the Uist Poetry, Dundee Law and The Blue Nib Chapbook competitions, and was runner-up in the Coast to Coast Chapbook competition. Stanza Festival commissioned a poem. Finola's work is widely published in *Gutter, Ofi Press, The Fenland Reed*, and *Firth*, among many other magazines and anthologies. Her first poetry pamphlet will be published by Red Squirrel Press in October 2019.

Elissa Soave is a Scottish writer whose work has appeared in *Structo, Open Pen, Gutter, Glasgow Review of Books*, and others. She is currently writing a novel which explores the themes of manipulation and revenge. She has also written three short plays.

Dan Spencer wrote "Our Common Areas" while living in Glasgow. He now lives in Osaka. His writing appears in *Gutter*, *Brittle Star* and *Flash: The International Short-Short Story Magazine*. In 2019, he has other upcoming pieces in *Stand*, *The Letters Page*, and *Flash*. **danspencerwriter.wordpress.com**

Iain Twiddy studied literature at university, and lived for several years in northern Japan. His poems have been published in *The London Magazine*, *The Poetry Review*, *Poetry Ireland Review*, *The Stinging Fly*, and elsewhere.

Lois Wappler is a poet from the North East of Scotland, currently in the final year of a BAH Literature degree. Her Doric work pays homage to the voice of the North East and gies it laldie on the page – nae apologetic apostrophes, jist Doric as it's spoken.

Lynnda Wardle was born Johannesburg. Her work has appeared in *Glasgow Review of Books*, *Gutter*, *New Orleans Review*, *New Writing Scotland*, *PENning* and *thi wurd*. She received a Creative Scotland New Writer's award (2007) and has just completed a memoir about being adopted and growing up in South Africa. **www.lynndawardle.com @lynndawardle5**

Helen Welsh is a food and drink blogger and part-time distillery tour guide. She lives in Fife, writes both fiction and non-fiction, and is planning another assault on the bracing world of self-publishing. She is a keen cook and would like to feed the world.

Mary Wight lives in the Scottish Borders. She holds an MSc in Creative Writing from the University of Edinburgh and has had poems published in magazines and anthologies, most recently in *Envoi*, *The Blue Nib*, *The Poets' Republic* and *Firth*.